To: Fareedah

Love and Gold

To my fellow Author...
You got this... I believe en you!

Keep going ♡

Christine Liverpool

ISBN: 978-1-387-87508-5

To Carol, Rodrick, Cindy, Lisa and Boots.
Thank you all for being there for me.

To Lawrence and Erin for telling me to hurry
and finish the book.

To homeyhill for the dope cover.

Thanks to everyone that asked when it will be done.
WE DID IT. Thank you all for believing in me. I
couldn't have done this without you I appreciate all
the support. PEACE and LOVE.

LT

Latanya "LT" Defreitas was born in the small village of Buxton in Guyana. Which is the only english speaking country in South America. Her mother and father were farmers in this village, where they raised chickens, goats, and hogs you name it. LT loved her animals like they were her own children. LT was an only child because her mother had lost her older brother during child birth six years prior to giving birth to her. So she cherished her baby girl more than life itself.

She taught her the value of life in many ways. The family came to America when LT was just fourteen years old. They moved to a small two bedroom apartment in South, Jamaica Queens. This was so LT could further her education. When LT got to America she didn't know what to make of it. Everyone spoke differently dressed differently and even acted differently from what she was used to.

She knew it would be an adjustment but nothing ever stopped LT from prevailing. She'd always been a people person so that was never the issue. Although the other kids teased her by making fun of her accent she never let them see her sweat. That Guyanese blood ran through her veins.

One day in math class a bully named Jade decided she would pick on LT. She started with her by saying her hair was fake because it was long and curly. LT had jet black hair that stopped in the middle of her back. Her family was amerindians which most Americans knew nothing about. But sure enough Jade was going to find out where her hair came from and her fighting skills.

Jade came over to LT's desk and pulled her hair, she was sure the weave ponytail would come right off and send the class in a frenzy.

Once that didn't work she began to talk about how LT was dressed. " who dressed you a farmer" she said mockingly. LT had on her favorite overalls that day she actually did bring from Guyana. The overalls reminded her of her animals that she missed oh so dearly. LT responded "Yea actually I am a farmer yuh skunt yuh".

Jade looked confused but from the disgust in LT's voice she gathered those weren't friendly words. As Jade stood there with a puzzled look on her face LT saw the perfect opportunity to rush her. She pounced on her so fast Jade never even saw it coming. LT grabbed her hair but the weave ponytail just came right off. She then reached for her neck. By the time Mr. Lawson heard the commotion and went to break it up LT had already given Jade a black eye.

The two were sent straight to the principles office. LT had never been suspended before because in Guyana you would get two lashes on your hands with a wild cane. When Lucinda LT's mother came to the school to pick her daughter up her first words to her were " yuh win right" in her thick Guyanese accent. LT replied "Ma I put a lickin' pon she". They both erupted in laughter as they drove home.

LT's mom knew how cruel kids could be she had her fair share of fights in Guyana when she was younger. Girls that looked like LT would always have a problem in school because she was naturally beautiful. Many of the girls in school wore a lot of make up fake hair and fake nails, so to see someone without it was like seeing a dog walking on its hind legs. When LT and her mom got home she was greeted by her beautiful brown and black yorkie boots.

She loved her puppy he was the only animal she could have in the apartment, so she treated him with as much love as she had her farm animals in Guyana. Boots was always there for LT. Her parents saw just how distraught LT was when she came to America so they came to a decision to get her a puppy. It was between that and a cat but they remembered how much LT disliked cats.

When she was just four years old she had her first and only encounter with the cat next door. Her name was mango she was a bright orange cat kind of like Garfield but the guyanese version. LT went over to the her friend cliff's house one day to play tag with him and some of the other kids in the village. She got to the top of the steps when Mango came charging at her like a bat out of hell before she could even react Mango was scratching her on her little chest she winced in pain and began to cry. Cliff heard what was going on and came to her rescue and slapped mango off of her.

Mrs. Thompson came out and asked LT if she was ok. LT replied "meh chest hurt me bad yuh know". Mrs. Thompson took LT inside there one bedroom home that she shared with her husband and two children Cliff and Christian. She put some aloe on LT's chest and blew on it. LT stopped crying as soon as the aloe touched the scratches. Mrs. Thompson didn't want any issues with Lucinda because the two went to school together she remembered the beating she put on another student in third form. When she cleaned LT up she then had to walk her home.

When LT and Mrs. Thompson got to the door Lucinda saw that LT had been crying she immediately asked "Is wha happen to you". Mrs. Thompson said when LT came to the door she startled her cat mango. So the cat attacked . Lucinda knew it was an accident but she told LT she couldn't go next door without her anymore. LT understood she told Mrs. Thompson thanks for walking her home. Lucinda then took LT inside the scratches were minor so she wasn't to upset.

When LT's dad came in from feeding the chickens she told him what had took place he tried not to get to furious because LT was standing right there. Linden Defreitas was a tall slim man with a dark brown complexion with large eyes that would brighten any room. He loved his daughter so much he felt like she was all he had in the world so even though it was a cat that hurt his daughter he saw red. Lucinda knew that look in his eyes all to well. Since having LT his temper had become much better. Linden was a hot head in his youth.

He was the act first think later kind of man. Then he met Lucinda the light skin buck girl is what he liked to call her because of her light complexion. They met at a party in Kitty, a small town in Guyana. Lucinda was there with a few friends Marcia, Sharlene, and Troy. They were more like sisters how long they knew one another. Linden saw Lucinda as soon as he walked in she lit up the party with her long golden curly locs.

He tried to think of how to get her attention. So he went with sending a drink for her and all of her friends. When the waiter came over with a round of shandy's for everyone the women were taken aback. The bartender said it came from the gentlemen in the blue shirt. They all looked over in unison. As he made his way over they all started laughing wondering who he was coming to speak to.

He walked over and said "hey Goldie locs I hope yuh like shandy". Lucinda blushed shyly as all her friends started to mock linden and call her Goldie locs. "I don't know how yuh know that but it happens to be my favorite". Lucinda said with a smile across her face. As he got closer the women moved out of the way so he could speak to Lucinda privately. "Do you dance". He asked. Lucinda loved dancing especially waltzing that was her favorite so when Beres Hammonds "I feel good" came on she seized the opportunity to show off her dancing skills.

Lucinda loved to waltz it was her favorite form of dancing. As the night came to a close Linden made sure to get her telephone number and walk her and her friends to the taxi stand. That was the day Linden and Lucinda became one.

THE MEETING

LT had been in America for 10 years before she met the man of her dreams Dean McKenner. She was on her way to the Bahamas for work as a flight attendant. While she was in Dunkin' Donuts that's when Dean first approached her. "Hello miss can I pay for your latte?" She pulled out her debit card and replied "thanks, but thank you".

This was all before she turned around and saw the most beautiful man she'd ever seen in her life. His smile was perfect. She instantly thought of those mentos commercials when the guy would smile with a mouth full of pearly white teeth. His complexion so smooth and silky it made her a little jealous. He had a fresh shape up it was out of this world, waves brushed at least 150 times for that morning.

LT Walked around Dean to exit the small Dunkin' Donuts in the airport. Dean then said "well can I walk you to your terminal miss". He patiently waited for a name that wouldn't come." Sure fella "she said. As they walked Dean asked her. "So miss do you have a name?". LT she said sternly. "Ok LT where are you flying to today?" She stopped in her tracks when he asked that.

"I'll be in the Bahamas today and where are you heading today sir". she inquired. "Will you look at that it's fate I'm heading to the Bahamas as well miss flight attendant LT" Dean stated in a smug tone and a devilish grin. She rolled her eyes but smiled on the inside just knowing she'd be seeing his beautiful smile and chocolate skin for three whole hours. "Why the eye roll miss LT.?" She just chuckled because he actually caught her.

."You can just call me LT and you are?". LT said as she changed the subject quickly. I'm Dean McKenner, Dean said ."Hello mr. Mckenner so what business do you have in the Bahamas and will Mrs. McKenner be joining you on this flight today." LT said hoping he would say no. He laughed knowing that LT was fishing but he took it as a compliment.

"There is no Mrs. McKenner yet I'm hoping that you can change that one day." He stated meaning every word. This made LT laugh out loud. She said "good one mr. McKenner ". "

Dean is fine Mr. Mckenner is my father." Dean exclaimed "Well when we get back to America do you think I can buy you a latte miss LT." She grinned again and said " maybe DEAN just maybe".

He knew then she was the one as soon as he saw her smile. He imagined how LT felt and even tasted. He just had to get her that latte first. "Well this is where I leave you mr. Dean". LT had to go start her shift she really loved her job getting to see the world while making money never hurt anyone.

She went down the passenger boarding bridge she told herself she wouldn't turn back, but she couldn't help herself she had to see that beautiful smile one last time. There he was standing at the gate smiling and waiving when she turned back she couldn't do anything but blush. When passengers were able to board LT had already told her friend and coworker Ariel about the handsome man who'd be boarding soon. When Ariel saw Dean she knew exactly what LT had been gushing about a few moments earlier. When all the passengers were seated LT made sure she did the in flight demonstration for safety in front of Dean so they could lock eyes.

When she was done picking up her pack off the floor. He leaned in and said "you can demonstrate on me anytime miss LT". She smiled and walked to the front of the plane where Ariel was already seated waiting to hear what was said by the Greek god who was seated in seat 8C. They both just laughed when LT finally sat down. "Girllll, Ariel said." That there is a beautiful man" LT joked and said

6

he's ok I guess" trying to downplay how handsome Dean actually was. But Ariel saw through her nonsense they'd been friends for so long they practically became sisters.

She loved Ariel like a sister. They'd been friends for 6 years the two were conjoined at the hip practically. When Ariel got married and had her daughter she saw no one more fit to be the godmother for her princess than LT. She remembered the day Ariel came over to her apartment and asked her to be the godmother she hugged her so tight and said "yes I'd be honored". A few months later they did the whole process and it was official LT was a proud God mother of a beautiful baby girl named Star.

"Earth to LT". Ariel said... So what's the next step with mr. Right in row 8?" "Here you go your planning a wedding in your head aren't you Ariel?" She knew Ariel like the back of her hand she saw the wheels turning in her head she probably had her dressed picked out knowing Ariel. He's cute and all but you know I'm still getting over Jason. Jason was Her high school sweetheart who thought it was ok to sleep with the neighbor and every woman he could find .

She wasn't ready just yet to jump right into a whole new relationship although she knew for a while it was over with Jason. He'd come in late smelling like perfume she'd never worn and started acting differently towards her. She tried her hardest to make it work with Jason she just knew they would end up married with children but it just wasn't in the cards for them.

As LT sat down getting ready for take off she thought about what Ariel said and knew she was right it was going on a year since the spilt with Jason but she was so focused on work and her business. LT wasn't just your average flight attendant.

Her mother came to America but still had that hustlers spirit in her. Her mom had taught LT everything she knew. Guyana was rich with gold her mother sold the farm when they were coming to America but not before she invested in the gold found in the "BUSH" that's what it was called. The resources in Guyana was hard to get a hold of if you were an outsider that's where LT came in she got in the "business" when she was just 22. Her business being bartering GOLD she was in the import/export business.

It started off small but when word spread that she was the best her business took off. LT gained many business partners doing her day job as a flight attendant. She'd see business men flying to Dubai, Milan everywhere imaginable she'd use her charm to see who was interested and she'd go from there. LT was indeed a business woman she had a way with words. Her tone was sultry and persuasive.

Men could never resist. She always made sure she kept things professional never got involved with clients. That's how she kept busy. She really didn't have time for a relationship. That was until Dean Mckenner took a trip to the Bahamas for work on that faithful day. LT nor Dean knew the exact role either would play in each others lives.

When they finally landed in the Bahamas Dean already had his card ready as he walked to the exit to the beautiful LT. He held up all the other passengers just to say to her. "miss LT here's my card cell phone included I sure hope I can buy you that latte before it gets to cold". LT couldn't help but smile. "We shall see Mr. Mckenner." And Just like that they parted ways.

LT had a business meeting to attend she had a twelve hour layover so she told Ariel she was going to her favorite little bar in the Bahamas. Ariel on the other hand had jet lag being a mom was already a full time job plus flying took all her energy. The two went to the hotel provided by the airline. LT showered and changed quickly she didn't want to have clients waiting to long. LT took a cab across town to a warehouse, from the outside it looked ran down and abandoned just how LT liked it.

"Hello gentleman" LT said as she entered the warehouse where six men were already seated. The men were all in awe of LT she had on a fitted red pants suit with black Christian loubitons they could see every curve under the suit she was wearing They didn't even care how late she was at this Point. "Sorry I'm late I got held up at the airport but I'm here now" LT said sensually. she could see all there eyes locked in on her at this moment.

"Shall we begin, Monroe sends his regards and apologizes for not making it to today's meeting. But I'm a fair woman so I'll give you all the deal of a lifetime." As they all came to an agreement on pricing and how much each man would take LT's thoughts drifted back to Dean. That was the day that changed her life forever.

DEAN

Dean McKenner was your typical all American. He was the poster boy for what a proud American was. He was born on a warm summer day on June 26,1983. His mother and father Carl and Camellia McKenner were originally from Savannah, Georgia, but moved to New York when Carl was promoted to lead detective. He was transferred to the 103rd precinct in Queens.

This was just two years before the two had their fourth and final child. The boy they'd been hoping for. Dean was born a whopping 9lbs 6oz. His mother just knew he was special. His three older sisters were so excited as they came rushing in through the doors of the LONG ISLAND JEWISH HOSPITAL.

When Erica, Lisa and Cynthia saw their baby brother they all had tears of joy. That was the day that changed all their lives. Unbeknownst to Camellia and her three daughters the day that had brought so much joy would also bring great devastation. On the other side of town while investigating the cartel Carl was involved in a sting that cost him his life. As the women in Carl's life waited for him to come to the hospital to meet his first born son Camellia felt like something was just not right.

That's when Detective Landry came into the hospital room to deliver the news. Camellia felt her heartbreaking into a million pieces. But she knew she had to be strong for her four children. The next day when Erica asked why her father hadn't come to see her little brother is when Camellia finally told them what had happened to there dad. The young women sobbed uncontrollably. Carl was laid to rest a week later. Dean never got to meet the hero that everyone called his father.

Although they lost Carl, Camellia made sure her children never wanted for anything. Dean always felt like he had to be the man of the house although he was the youngest person in the household. Every single one of camellias children never received anything less than a A in any class. Dean being the only boy in the house played every sport. His mother made sure Dean did whatever made him happy. Her daughters all took turns watching over their little brother.

When Dean made football captain at AUGUST MARTIN HIGH SCHOOL it came as no surprise to his mother or siblings. The homecoming game is where everything changed for him in his senior year. As the crowd fell silent after the snap Dean's offense fell short. he didn't see the 275 pound senior from JAMAICA HIGH SCHOOL rushing towards him. When he finally saw him he was already on top of Dean. The way the two boys landed left Dean's arm broken in three places.

Dean always felt like football was his everything. While in the hospital he was born in his mother Camellia walked in the room to see her baby boy. She immediately broke down in tears. Just the mere thought of her one and only son being hurt broke her spirit. She knew she had to be strong for him so she pulled herself together.

As camellia pulled up a chair to be close to her baby boy a single tear fell from his eye. "Mom this is it I just know it." Dean said sounding defeated. "What have I alway told you Dean" his mother questioned. Dean looked his mother in the eyes and said "everyone gets knocked down, so you can choose to stay there and wallow or you can stand up and face another day".

"That's my baby, we can't let this minor set back stop you." Camellia said with a smile on her face. Dean couldn't help but smile his mother had a way of making any situation seem like it didn't even matter. She was so strong not just for Dean but for his sisters as well. When the doctor walked in Camellia was feeding Dean some jello. She sat the red cup down so she could listen to what the doctor had to say about her sons injury. Dr. Calloway got right to it.

"Hello mrs. McKenner, hello Dean I hope your stay is going well so far." He said trying to lighten the mood. They both gave him a dry smile. He realized this wasn't his crowd. It looks as though you have a broken radius and your ulna is fractured, you took a hard hit young man." As camellia sat there listening she could tell Dean would take this hard football was his first love.

"Your arm will take about six months to heal completely. You'll be in therapy a few times a week. You can attend school in about four weeks. Dr. Calloway explained to Dean and camellia. I'm sorry this happened to you my son always tells me about how great you are. I know this is a minor setback but it isn't over until it's over." The doctor said trying to sound optimistic.

Dean just laid there feeling defeated. His mother had to get to work she was the head surgeon at Mount Sinai hospital. She kissed Dean on the forehead and told him Cynthia would bring him a change of clothes. Dean just laid there thinking of what could have been. The coaches from OHIO STATE and DUKE were both in attendance. He just felt like a failure.

While he drifted off a light knock came on the door. It was Stephanie his girlfriend. She stood in the doorway with a bouquet of flowers and five balloons that said get well soon. Dean smiled. Stephanie began to cry. He told her "please don't cry babe I'll be fine". She just couldn't help it she knew how much football meant to Dean. She walked in sat the flowers down and gave Dean a kiss.

"Everyone is so worried Dean" she said with sadness in her voice. "I broke my arm, I'll live." Dean said trying to make light of the situation. "But the scouts". She began to say until she saw the pained look on Deans face. "You know what tell me what you want to eat, I know hospital food can be a drag I'll go get it for you." Stephanie said eager to please her boyfriend. Dean just really wanted to be alone with his thoughts so he just said a frosty from Wendy's. "Well my man gets what my man wants" she stated with optimism.

As Stephanie was heading out of the room she ran into Deans older sister Cynthia. "Hey Stephanie how are you doing?" Cynthia questioned "I'm okay, it's your brother I'm worried about". She said while she looked back in the room at Dean. "He will be okay that one there is trooper always has been always will be". Cynthia said with a smile on her face.

"I'll see you when I get back the patient requested a frosty" Stephanie exclaimed. The two exchanged a little chuckle because Dean really loved a frosty. When Cynthia saw her brother she was instantly reminded of her dad. Dean looked just like him. She began to cry. "Not you too Cyn, I can't take anymore tears for the day please." Dean stated trying not to sound like a complete jerk. "I'm sorry baby brother this just sucks I know how hard you've been working, and practicing all summer". Cyn said with sadness in her voice. They both fell silent. That's when Dean started laughing uncontrollably. Cynthia couldn't figure out what had her brother cracking up.

Dean couldn't control himself at this point. "What's so funny". Cynthia asked her brother. "This is one of the worse days of my life sis, and all I can think about is a frosty from Wendy's." Dean said while still laughing. Cyn joined in on his laughter. "Listen Dean this isn't the end, you're an intelligent young man, I know because I helped raised you. Cyn said. She continued with "I've watched you for the past seventeen years turn into a great man like dad. Although you never got a chance to meet him you are him and he is you.

That was the moment it came to Dean he'd become a police officer just like his dad. He'd carry on his fathers legacy. At first his mother and sisters weren't to sure but once Dean put his mind to something that was it. There was no turning back he focused on whatever had his attention. He was a go getter and this was his new obsession. Straight out of college Dean went to the police academy. He was excelling in everything they threw at him. He was a man on a mission. A mission to make his father proud.

Dean was promoted to detective in no time. His dedication to the job was undeniable. The fact that his father died a hero helped just a bit. The captain at the time happened to be Carl's partner Ralph Sterling. He did indeed have a soft spot for Dean, he felt obligated to his partner to look over his son he never knew. Dean didn't make it hard at all. He was always eager to learn more about the job and also learn about his father in the process. It was a win-win. Captain Sterling took Dean under his wing. They'd discuss past cases that Deans father worked on. It's like Dean saw the world through his fathers eyes. He loved every minute of it.

A few months before Dean made detective his mom was diagnosed with Breast cancer. The children were distraught. Deans sisters were all married and living out of state. They all came together once the news got out about their mother. As they all stood around there mom she woke up. She hadn't had all her children in one place since her daughters all moved out. Dean just couldn't leave his mom, not because he couldn't afford to but because she'd never been alone. Dean always felt like the man of the house.

When Camellia finally registered that all of her children were there with her she cried tears of joy. "All my babies in one place what more could a mother ask for. She beamed with excitement in her tone. They all breathed a sigh of relief just to hear there mom lively and happy made them happy as well. Camellia was a strong woman she wouldn't let something like cancer stand in her way she ended up beating the cancer like it stole something.

When Dean met LT for the first time it was like nothing he'd ever felt before. She was like a chocolate angel. He didn't care if she shot him down he was giving it a shot. The day she called was one he'd never forget. "Hi is this Mr. Mckenner?" The sultry voice came through Dean's phone. She'd taken two weeks to call so Dean gave up hope. "Why yes it is." Dean replied still not sure who it was on the other line. "Well then I believe you owe me a latte". LT said while smirking into the phone. Dean lit up when he finally realized it was the most beautiful flight attendant he'd seen.

"You just give me a time and place, mrs. LT." He said. That was the first of many lattes to come. Dean was so caught up in his career he never thought of taking anyone serious. That was until Latanya Defreitas came into his life. He'd never felt the way he felt about her about any woman he'd ever been with. They'd been spending a lot of time together when Dean finally asked LT to be official with him. She was hesitant at first because of her break up that she couldn't shake. But with Dean everything felt different almost to good to be true.

The two became one they even moved in together. Although LT knew Dean was a detective she still stayed knowing what it could one day mean for her business on the side. She made sure she moved carefully. Dean was none the wiser. Dean just knew he'd do any and everything for this woman who'd one day be his wife.

ARIEL

Ariel did a light jog to the preschool her daughter Star was attending. She was just a few minutes late. She got so caught up cleaning the home they lived in with her husband Lane. They'd been together for eight years he was a real estate broker and she was his sexy and beautiful flight attendant. They'd met at a diner in Memphis Tennessee.

That's where Ariel was originally from she was there visiting her mom and dad when she stopped in the local diner SWEETS & THANGS. When a stranger said to her "excuse me mam what's good here to eat?" When she turned around and saw the clean well groomed specimen standing in front of her with a custom made blue tailored suit with green eyes so piercing she felt like he could see right through her soul. She was speechless.

Lane stood 6 feet flat his stature was one of a man who had once played football maybe in his college years with light skin and a goatee on his well rounded face. As Ariel stood there at a lost for words Lane saw his chance to get a little closer to the slender beauty that stood just a few feet away.

Ariel was 5'8 and slim her complexion sun kissed with a copper undertone. She had a blonde and brown curly weave in that matched her hazel eyes. Ariel got a little flustered she felt as though she wasn't looking her best she had on her old college t-shirt and some destructive jeans, with her old Jordan's she'd been reunited with when she made it to her home town. She was there for a few days her dad just had open heart surgery and she couldn't imagine losing him so she flew home as soon as she could. Lane had his hand out for about a minute when he finally just took Ariel's into his own.

He was hoping the gesture didn't scare off the young lady he couldn't take his eyes off of since he walked in the little mom and pop diner. "Hi sweetheart I'm Lane Cassidy and you are?" Lane said in his New York accent. Ariel had a southern drawl she couldn't hide even if she wanted to. "Hi I'm Ariel brown sir it's so great to meet you mr. Cassidy" Ariel said in her thick Tennessee accent. When Lane heard it he chuckled a little. Ariel looked at him curiously and asked. "What's the matter Mr. Lane did I do something wrong."

He was used to New York women being so aggressive and tough to see someone so gentle and calling him sir was new to him he was just taken aback. "No, no mrs. Brown" he said hoping she'd correct him. She did just that "it's miss Brown" Ariel stated with a huge smile across her face. Lane couldn't believe someone so beautiful could not be married. This was his chance to ask her out but the conversation was interrupted by a car honking. It was her brother Schiller holding on the horn of their parents Chevy Tahoe.

He witnessed his sister talking to the man in the suit. He'd always embarrass Ariel, but it was their thing she would do the same when a girl was around. Lane looked outside and said to Ariel. "Well I know it isn't your husband but your boyfriend surely doesn't want you talking to me". Ariel just looked at her brother and motioned for him to cut it out while smiling. That's my little brother Mr. Cassidy he's just being a little jerk because a man as handsome as yourself is talking to his older sister, you see it's a game we play with one another we may be just a little to old Now". Ariel said coyly.

Her face flushed with embarrassment her freckles as red as the apple in Snow White. Lane let out a sigh of relief. Well miss Brown I'll let you get back to it I'll be in Tennessee for three more days then I'm heading back to New York on Saturday the eighth. "I hope you can squeeze me in darling". He said mimicking her southern accent. She couldn't help but laugh at Lane being silly. "I think I can son" Ariel surprised him with the knowledge of New York slang. She was just full of surprises Lane couldn't wait to really get to know her his southern bell. The two exchanged numbers and went along there way. When Ariel got in the car she punched her brother in the arm. Schiller said to her "Did I scare Mr. Blue suit Ari". Which he called her because he couldn't pronounce Ariel when he was just a boy so it just stuck with him. "No thankfully". Ariel exclaimed.

He's a New Yorker and so dreamy. They drove back to the house that their parents lived in. They were the youngest two of four children for Mr. and Mrs. Brown. Her two older siblings Scott and Dante were in the military they couldn't get leave in time to come see their dad after his surgery. As they entered the home laughing they were met by their mother telling them to quiet down because their father was asleep .

She looked sleep deprived she hadn't been sleeping well since her husband fell ill. "Momma please get some rest we've got it from here" Ariel pleaded. As much as Joyce wanted to say no her body needed it. She agreed and headed upstairs to the master bedroom. As Schiller and Ariel walked to the kitchen they could hear their father coughing.

They dropped their bags on the counter and ran in to see Charles laughing at the contestants on "Let's make a deal". Dad are you alright Schiller asked. His father looked at him and said sternly. "This is the best I've ever felt". They all erupted in laughter. "Momma said you were asleep daddy" Ariel stated in a low tone. I faked it your momma looked like the walking dead, she was looking like she did surgery right along with me." Chuck stated "she can't take care of me if she's not well or getting rest, I'm glad you all came when you did so you could actually guilt her up those stairs".

Ariel decided to give Lane a call the biggest smile crept across his face when he heard the beauty from SWEETS AND THANGS on the other end of his phone. "I thought this was one of my Nashville associates when I saw the 615 area code but boy am I glad it's you instead". Lane said as he breathed a sigh of relief on the other end of the phone. So miss Ariel can I take you out to dinner or is that to forward?". Lane asked hoping for a yes. Ariel's freckles turned pink as she blushed on the phone with the gorgeous stranger. "I'd love to Lane but my dad isn't really well right now, is there anyway we can reschedule for another time?". Ariel exclaimed.

Lane was a bit disappointed he couldn't see the lovely young woman but he knew not to push to hard. "Okay another time then" he said trying not to sound so defeated. After Ariel hung up from Lane she could hear her father chuck call her from the living room he was confined to. She ran in to check on her father. "Yes daddy" she said. "Ariel did I hear correctly was that you on the phone turning down a date because I'm not well" chuck said with a stern look on his face. Ariel was left shocked.

She didn't know her father could hear her conversation she was a little embarrassed. "Listen young lady I have your mother and brother here you have done more than enough you've already traveled all the way from New York City to be with your old man, you deserve to paint the town red on your last night here. Chuck said to her while looking her in the eyes.

She did want to see Lane again he was quiet the looker the more she thought about him. She stepped onto the porch of the family home to call Lane back. He'd saved her number already so he answered knowing exactly who it was this time. "Miss Ariel two calls in one day I feel so honored I hope this means you've changed your mind and this date is going to happen after all". Lane pleaded. "Why yes it is...your dreams are coming true today, sir." She said jokingly. Lane couldn't help but laugh at what he was hearing.

"Well Call me lucky, what's a good place to take a beautiful woman out here you know us New Yorkers love southern food." Lane stated with a cheesy smile to go with the cheesy line he knew he just said. That was just the first of many the two had been dating for only six months when Lane proposed. He told his mother he just knew this was the woman he wanted to spend the rest of his life

19

with. Mrs. Roland had never seen her son so smitten with any girl he'd brought home before.

Lane took Ariel back to where it all started. The Tennessee restaurant SWEETS & THANGS. He even managed to get her mother, father, and brother Schiller to attend the engagement. When the two walked in and Ariel saw her family she finally realized something was up. When she turned back Lane was already on one knee. She immediately started crying. The emotions just took over.

Lane looked her right in her eyes and said. "Ariel Brown, from the time I asked you what was good here six months ago I've realized I found someone I've been missing my whole life. Your the most kind, generous and loving person I've ever met. Will you make me the happiest man in the world and be my wife." Ariel's hazel eyes were filled with tears of joy as she said "YES LANE, YES A MILLION TIMES." The two wed six months later.

The honeymoon was in Cabo San Lucas, MEXICO. It was Ariel's first time making love but she was so ready. Lane brought her through the threshold of there hotel room. She was living the fairytale she always wanted. They drew a bath because the flight was delayed. They were a little tired but Ariel wouldn't let that stop her from pleasing her husband. When they finished the bath Ariel stayed in the bathroom to put on the lingerie she'd bought for this occasion.

When she opened the door and walked through the hallway to get back to the bedroom Lane was laying in the bed waiting. When he looked up and saw Ariel in an all white corset with matching panties with white fishnet stockings. Lane became instantly erect. He didn't think Ariel had it in her because she was so conservative. She even made a playlist for the occasion. TREY SONGZ neighbors know my name started playing on the Harmon Bluetooth speaker she brought along with her.

As she made her way over to the bed she crawled over to Lane on the king sized danish modern bed provided by the hotel. Lane just watched her. His wife, his love, his heart in human form. She stood up and did a little sexy dance for her man. This lasted about two minutes because Lane wanted nothing more than to taste his wife. He grabbed her and pulled her close and kissed her passionately. He then slid her panties off with his mouth. Ariel didn't say a word. He then opened her legs and smiled and licked his lips. Ariel had only read books and looked at a few pornos. But this was an outer body experience for her.

Lane was down there for a good half an hour making sure his wife felt the pleasure she deserved. Ariel didn't know what to do she brought Lane up to her lips and kissed him. She could taste herself on his lips. Lane then got on top and slid inside Ariel just slow enough not to hurt her but enough so he could feel the warmth and tightness of his virgin wife. As the two became one a single tear fell from Ariel's eyes. She wasn't crying because of pain. She was crying because she was so happy that she'd saved herself for a true love.

The moment was perfect and everything she'd imagined it would be. As they finished the second round Lane couldn't stop staring at his beautiful wife. Ariel just giggled as she stared into her husbands eyes. "What's so funny babe?" Lane questioned his blushing wife. Ariel simply replied "Lane you're everything I've ever hoped and dreamed of and more, you know you're all that and a bag of chips." The two laughed hysterically from the corny joke she'd said as they drifted off to sleep.

The rest of the honeymoon consisted of clubbing, dune buggies and a lot of alcohol. They really enjoyed themselves. She couldn't wait to get back to work to tell her best friend LT all the details. They kept nothing from one another or so she thought. "LT he is amazing in every aspect". Ariel gushed about the man she called her husband. LT was genuinely happy for her friend she deserved happiness.

Lane and Ariel became inseparable. Only six months into the marriage they found out they were having a baby girl. Ariel couldn't believe she was pregnant. She was flooded with emotions leaving the doctors office. She was excited but mostly terrified. She called her best friend LT. "Hey girl are you busy can I stop by?" Ariel said into her phone. LT could hear it in her voice something was off with her friend. "I'm here I just finished working out, come over in ten minutes Ari." LT said.

Ariel drove over to LT's apartment she felt so relieved to see her face. LT was the one person who could calm Ariel down without even trying. It was something about her demeanor and persona that calmed anyone. She'd learned that at a young age. Calmness during a crisis. As Ariel sat down on LT's couch she could see the concern on Latanyas face. "I know I'm scaring you, LT I'm so afraid but it a good way." Ariel stated. With a confused look on her face LT put it all together and said "you're pregnant aren't you?" Ariel burst into tears. Tears of joy the two women were overwhelmed with joy.

"Ariel you scared me with the way you were sounding on the phone." LT explained. "I'm so sorry girl I didn't know who else to call, Lane doesn't know as yet." Ariel said with a confused look on her face. She wanted to tell him in a special way something he'd always remember. So the two came up with a plan. When Lane came home that evening their were two teddy bears in the couch. One with a pink bow and the other with a blue one. He was so confused. He didn't know what was going on.

Ariel made him his favorite dish. Baked ziti with garlic bread. He knew something was up. When she came out the bedroom and saw her man, her king she broke down crying. All the emotions took over. She wanted it to be special but couldn't control her hormones. "Baby what's wrong is everything ok?" Lane questioned. Ariel said "we're going to be parents babe, like a mother and father". She couldn't even get her words in order. He couldn't stop kissing his wife and kissing her stomach. This was the second best day of his life. The first was when she agreed to marry him.

LANE

Lane had a rough upbringing. His parents were killed in a car crash when he was just six years old. He was in and out of foster homes. He was destined to be a product of his environment. But Lane never let his circumstances define him. He lived in abusive homes and neglectful homes until he finally found the right one. It was a couple who couldn't conceive. The Roland's They loved Lane from the first time they laid eyes on him.

His case worker had explained to the couple the hardships young Lane had faced while being in the system. They were determined to help the young man and mold him into a great man. When Lane first got to there home he was shy and a little nervous. When they showed him his room he was in disbelief. The full size bed, the flat screen, and a PlayStation. He'd only played it at one of his classmates homes. He was happy but still reserved.

As they all sat for dinner that evening Lane said something that took the Roland's by surprise. "Will you guys keep me?" Young Lane asked his foster parents. The Roland's looked at one another. Mrs. Roland answered in the sweetest way. "Lane I wasn't able to carry a child of my own, so god brought you here for us. So I won't let him or you down". This brought a smile to his face. They were genuine people. Although Lane was only ten at the time he knew this was his home. He wouldn't let anything mess that up.

When Lane entered high school he kept his grades up. He was on the honor roll but he fell into a bad crowd. He never actually fit in. So when the popular kids took a liking to him he was all for it. He started off with skipping school, Going to parties coming in late and disobeying his curfew. He started to get out of control. He was losing his way. His parents never treated him badly. He just felt like he'd never live up to there standards.

The night of the spring formal is when everything turned around for him. Lane and a couple of other students were in the parking lot at Hillcrest high school smoking weed. They were all standing around cracking jokes on what everyone was wearing and which girls looked good in the school. None of them saw when the cop come up behind them. Someone had reported them saying students were smoking on school property. Lane was so scared he was already on thin ice at home. His parents loved him unconditionally but he was becoming a handful.

They all were taken to central bookings. When Mr. and Mrs. Roland showed up they had a look of disappointment Lane knew all to well. This was the last time they warned. Because he was two weeks away from turning eighteen he wasn't going to be charged in criminal court for possession. The police were ready to throw the book at him. They looked at his record and they were ready to send him to a juvenile detention center. His parents explained to the officers Lanes past.

Detective Mckenner had a son on the way so he felt sympathy for the kid. Mr. Roland tried to explain to them that Lane wasn't a bad kid. He was just going through the motions of growing up without his real parents. They all decided to teach Lane a lesson and make him do community service at his school. They put him in a jumpsuit and made him clean up the school. This was exactly what he needed. The possibility of him going to jail scared him straight. He didn't even mind the embarrassment.

That was the day Lane decided he'd turn his life all the way around. He felt like he dodged a bullet. He began realtor school the next year. He was a smooth talker and he wanted to follow in his father James Roland's footsteps. His father couldn't be more proud when Lane received his real estate license. He was just a natural he closed his first home while shadowing his dad. This was his calling he enjoyed it.

When LT and Dean started dating Ariel set up a double date so they all could meet. She loved setting up dinner parties and outings. They all met at BKNY, a Thai restaurant on Francis Lewis boulevard. Ariel and lane arrived first. She wanted to make a good impression on detective Dean. When they walked in Lane felt like he'd seen Dean before. When Dean introduced himself it hit Lane like a ton of bricks. "You're detective mckenners son?" Lane questioned. Dean was puzzled. He'd actually never met his dad, he told everyone about his dads passing on the day he was born.

Thats when Lane told them all about how his dad saved his life from going to shit. The world was so small. They were all destined to meet. Dean and Lane had an instant connection from then on.

He told Dean how he looked just like his father. Dean heard that his whole life. When dinner was over Lane felt compelled to get to know Dean. He just wanted to look over the mans son that looked out for him. They became great friends. They went to basketball games together fishing trips and double dates the women set up. It was a great friendship the men got along and so did there women. Lane finally felt like he had a family of his own.

WEDNESDAY

As LT was about to finish up the dishes she could hear Dean call her from the bedroom. She tried to ignore him because she could also hear Sean T in the living room on the television. It was after all WEDNESDAY or workout Wednesday as LT called it. After she couldn't ignore Dean any longer she finally made her way to the bedroom. She stood in the doorway 5'6 medium build with curves in all the right places, with her long black curly hair in a loose ponytail wearing her pink and black yoga pants with a matching sports bra.

Dean looked up and saw her, he couldn't even remember his train of thought as he stared at the love of his life. LT stood there confused and slightly annoyed and said "yes Dean what is so urgent that you couldn't stop yelling my name out you know it's Wednesday babe". He just sat there in awe of the woman who stood before him.

Dean walked over to LT grabbed her by the neck gentle enough not to hurt her but just rough enough for her to know what was about to go down. Dean was 6'5 with the build of a god a six pack that showed just how much he loved the gym, with smooth dark chocolate skin his hair cut low with deep waves even the ocean was jealous . His Colgate smile always made it hard for LT to ever say no to him .

He kissed LT while his hand was still around her neck he used his free hand to glide slowly down her body, slow enough to make all the hairs on her body rise. LT got upset and tried to fight him off just a little because she actually wanted to work out. But who was she kidding this was a work out in the making. As LT tried to push Dean away his grip got a little tighter on her neck.

She could never resist him for too long, He was indeed her kryptonite. She tried to speak in a raspy voice "Dean its Wednesday". Dean slipped his hand into her yoga pants, with one hand still around her neck LT let out a soft moan as she tried to fight back. Dean knew at that moment he had her right where he wanted her.

As he motioned his hand up and down ,around and around the lips of her vagina she could feel the first orgasm of many coming for that evening. LT finally pushed him off of her He licked his fingers slowly flashing those pearly whites that she just loved . LT felt like he had one up on her so she slipped out of her yoga pants. She walked seductively to the bed and asked in a raspy voice "you coming". Dean was there in 2.5 seconds, in her head LT thought my turn.

She pushed Dean on the bed slowly as she pulled down his Nike basketball shorts to see an already erect penis. She smiled devilishly. She began to kiss him deeply... then used her tongue as she made her way down his body . She could hear Deans breathing get a little louder. LT thought to herself: Ha I bet you wished you let me work out....She finally made it to that special place... she placed her mouth on his penis, first she started off slowly as she got into the groove her pace picked up.

She could hear Dean panting for dear life "LT, LT....LATANYA" as he exploded inside her warm mouth. Dean was always amazed when LT showed her oral sex skills but this time she took it to another level. Being the MAN in the relationship he always felt strange when his toes curled. He looked down at LT and a smirk came across her face so seductively it made him instantly ready again. He grabbed her so quickly she didn't even realize she was sitting on his face. As they developed a rhythm Deans tongue maneuvred UP and Down side to side around in a circle. He could feel LT's legs clench his face he knew exactly how to please his woman.

He lifted her up right when she was about to climax. Her face turned so red she looked like a Marciano cherry. He then slid inside her slowly so she could feel every 10 inches of him inside of her. For LT every time felt like the first time she felt this bliss. She moved her hips slowly up and down. Dean wanted to watch her as she orgasmed all over him. As LT climaxed Dean could feel himself coming as well.

The two came in unison like two souls intertwined. As they laid there no one saying a word they both knew what the other was thinking, which was that was simply amazing. LT had long forgotten about Sean T playing in the living room as she initiated round two of the sexual escapades on that wonderful Wednesday evening. "I'm famished Dean". LT pouted as she stared at Dean hoping he would get up to make them his famous grilled cheese sandwiches.

"Those two sessions gave you quiet an appetite huh" Dean said with a sly smile. They both laughed as he got up to make those sandwiches and thinking how much more perfect his life could be. As Dean stood over the stove making the grilled cheese LT sat at the dining room table going over her schedule for work. Being a flight attendant was the second best thing in her life after Dean of course. Dean walked over with two plates in his hands.

LT could smell the aroma of melted mozzarella cheese her favorite. She had the biggest smile plastered on her face. Dean couldn't help but let out a laugh. "What's so funny babe" LT asked a bit confused. "Hun you have to see the kool aid smile on your face right now it's the cutest and funniest thing".

Dean explained while trying not to laugh anymore. "Oh hush Dean you know how I feel about your grilled cheese sandwiches" LT said with a smile across her face. "You know I can also make real food too?" Said Dean as he placed LT's plate in front of her. She dug right in ignoring his last statement. Her love for his grilled cheese was real.

As they sat there enjoying each other's company Dean realized he wouldn't want to be sitting there enjoying grilled cheese sandwiches with anyone else. It was time to ask the woman of his dreams to marry him. First he'd start with a ring he'd asked her early on in the relationship what was her dream wedding ring and she told him he couldn't afford it jokingly. It was a princess cut ring with a blue diamond like the one the old lady threw into the sea at the end of titanic.

LT just loved Titanic well not the tragic ending but the love story within the tragedy. Dean knew this so beginning tomorrow he'd go out and get her ring. Then the hard part would be asking her father for her hand in marriage. LT's father was so protective over his baby girl Dean was worried what he would say. Dean knew all about Jason the guy who broke LT's heart prior to them dating and so did mr. Defreitas. Dean decided to focus on the ring for now.

"Dean what are you thinking about I've been having a conversation with myself for the past five minutes. LT asked as she snapped her fingers in the air trying to get Deans attention. "Sorry babe I was thinking about the case I'm working on" Dean lied. "Don't let the case consume you babe I know how you get when you let your job get to you". She said sternly as she got up from the table to go wash the plates.

Dean followed when she placed the dishes in the sink Dean started to kiss on her neck slowly. He knew the exact spot that sent LT into a frenzy. She slipped out of her panties that she'd been walking around in as Dean took off his boxers. He bent her over as he entered her nice and slow. As they got into a rhythm Dean could feel LT's orgasm coming he held off on his own because he wanted her to enjoy every minute of it. As he felt her knees buckle his orgasm came shortly after.

Dean lifted LT up and told her the dishes could wait he took her to the shower where they would finished there love making until they finally went to bed that evening.

Dean fell asleep first LT just stared at this beautiful man god sent to her. She couldn't help but imagine being married to him and one day having his children. But that was for another day she kissed Dean on the cheek and fell into a well deserved slumber.

THE CASE

As Dean sat at his desk replaying last nights events with LT he could feel himself getting erect all over again. LT had that effect on him. They'd been dating for almost 3 years now. He just knew she was the one. "Mckenner, MCKENNER" a voice yelled. It was captain Casey. "Earth to detective DEAN MCKENNER".

Dean hadn't realized his day dream was distracting him from doing actual work. "Oh hey captain" he said as he snapped back to reality. "It Must've been a great night you're smiling from ear to ear" said Casey. Casey was a tall slender black man in his mid fifties he'd been on the force 23 years and made captain 3 years prior. He took a liking to Dean he reminded him of himself when he first made detective 15 years ago.Dean sat up and asked "what's going on captain".

Casey started to speak when Sargent Timothy stokes walked up. "I have a source that came up with some intel on Monroe". He had Deans full attention now. Dean had been searching for Monroe for 5 years he was ready to take the son of a bitch down. There was a silent trade going on for years Dean had been investigating he just knew he was going to catch the man they called "MONROE". "What do you have sarge" Dean said. Timothy fixed his tie and began to speak.

"Well the source says they have a meeting in the caymans on the eleventh". That's five days away said Dean. Well you better get your sunscreen ready captain Casey said. "I'm going" Dean stated. This is the break he'd been waiting for. But what would he tell LT it was there third year anniversary on the 12th as well. He just knew she'd be pissed but this was his job. "I'm on it captain" he said with the utmost confidence.

He'd deal with LT when he got home later. Ramirez came walking over to Deans desk with a latte and a coffee with two creams and a one sugar as Dean liked it. Ramirez had been Dean's partner for over a year and she got used to him obsessing over cases. Jessica Ramirez was a cop in the Dominican Republic for five years before she came to America. She was five eight with curly sandy blonde hair with an hour glass shape that showed through her pants suit.

All the men in the precinct couldn't help but stare any time she walked in. But in reality she just wasn't interested in men. She'd dated them but it was always something missing. Being a lesbian was frowned upon in her country. When she came to America and saw how accepting they were here she finally felt at ease and could live the life she always knew she wanted.

She'd just made detective a year prior so Dean was a mentor of hers she'd admired him he was like the big brother she always wished she'd had. "Hey McKenner I got your fix" she said jokingly. Dean looked up and smiled as Ramirez passed him his coffee. "I hope Nalini won't mind you have a trip coming up." Dean explained. Ramirez took a sip of her latte and asked about the trip Dean was referring to. "Casey just told me about a lead on Monroe in the Cayman Islands.

"So pack your sunscreen we'll be going on a little trip." Said Dean. "Nalini knows I have work what she won't like is the fact I'm going to the Caymans without her". Ramirez stated. As they both laughed at the fact she'd get an earful later on. "Well now that, that's out of the way we can talk a little more unofficial business." Dean said with a huge smile on his face. Ramirez knew he was going to talk about LT that smile only came across his face when he spoke about her. "What's up partner what's going on?" Ramirez inquired.

"I'm going to ask LT to marry me it's been on my mind so much it's like a voice is yelling at me what are you waiting for". Dean said with the biggest smile on his face. "Now if we could catch this bastard Monroe it would just be the cherry on top." He added. The two got a kick out of that one.

JASON

LT was on her way home from work on the other side of town. LT loved to travel Since she was a little girl her mom would take her on trips all over the world. She was trying to figure out how she would tell Dean she had to work for Ariel on there anniversary she knew Dean would be a little angry but Ariel had an appointment with her baby girl this gave LT the perfect opportunity to go to the Cayman Islands where she had a meeting scheduled. As she drove down the Long Island expressway bumping her favorite artist ROWE OneTen.

She heard a familiar voice that always brought a smile to her face. Her childhood friend Bill blast was on the Intro. They had all grew up together but unfortunately Bill passed away. Thanks to her Good friend Rowe he lived on forever in his music. As she cruised through traffic listening to the GOLD RUSH album she didn't even realize she almost missed her exit she switched lanes right in time. As she drove down liberty or "little Guyana" as she called it she stopped in one of her favorite Guyanese restaurants BROWN BETTY for the best chicken fried rice in the world she just couldn't resist.

She made sure to grab Dean a plate as well, he had become hooked since they started dating she remembered him telling her "I don't think I'm eating American food ever again". She laughed at the thought while she ordered. As she walked out she ran into someone she was hoping to never see again her ex Jason. "As I live and breathe if it isn't LaTanya D." Jason said with a huge smile on his face.

"Hello Jason, Goodbye Jason" LT said with annoyance in her tone. Jason stood there puzzled as if he forgot all the times he cheated on her and what he put her through. LT didn't forget any of those nights she stayed up crying or any of the times he'd come home after cheating on her smelling like the next woman. LT began to walk away but Jason was persistent. "LaTayna why are you in such a hurry I've missed you I can't believe we haven't spoken in so long". Jason exclaimed.

LT couldn't believe what she was hearing. She had to admit the time apart really did Jason some justice he still had the bluest eyes with that curly brown hair. He was 6'3 so he towered over LT he looked like he started hitting the gym more he looked well put together. Jason's parents were Guyanese as well so they simply adored LT. When his mother found out they broke up because her son couldn't keep it in his pants she smacked him with a pointer broom.

She even went as far as to call LT and beg her for another chance, as if it were her relationship to salvage. LT remembered the conversation like it was yesterday. "Latanya I don't know wuh wrong wid mi son, he's just like his blasted fadda, dey wan run round run round and ain Kay who deh hurt in the wake of deh destruction". She said with disdain in her voice towards her son. "Mrs. Campbell I'm sorry you felt the need to call me although I do appreciate everything you've done for me while I was with your son, I just can't continue to be disrespected and hurt anymore, it's only so much a girl can take".

Deidre Campbell was so proud of LT at that moment she only had two words to say to her . "You're right". She came from a time when once a man was taking care of his main family the women allowed anything. The women on the side and the children that came with them. So to see LT so young and strong it made her so proud. She'd only wish she had that strength to walk away from Jason's father who had Seven children outside of there marriage.

"Latanya, I just wish mi son see in yuh wah I do, your an amazing young lady and I see nothing but good things for you in the future." She stated. LT felt the tears coming down she'd grown so fond of Deirdre. She said her goodbyes and that was the day she knew it was really over with Jason. "Hello, LATANYA" she heard Jason saying as he snapped his finger in her face trying to get her attention. LT snapped out of her trance. "I'm not doing this with you today Jason". She said as she walked away from her ex lover.

He was her first love so that pain never really went away she did a good job at avoiding him but she knew this day was inevitable. Jason did a light jog and caught up to her. She could feel her face getting hot. "How can I help you what more do you want from me". She questioned. "One drink its all I ask of you". He said pleading at this point.

"Fine Jason,Fine." LT gave in only because he wouldn't take no for an answer. "Friday at SOCO in Brooklyn meet me there" he said "I know your man probably doesn't want me around but this is just two old friends catching up". Jason stated with a sly smile across his face. With all that was going on LT had forgotten about Dean in that moment. "I have to go like RIGHT NOW". She said as she walked over to her car.

Jason had this effect on her that she just couldn't say no to him. Although she wanted closure she still had to think about how Dean would react to all of this. She'd tell him when she got home and see what he made of all of this. As she drove home she couldn't believe that Jason still made her feel like her younger self. She loved Dean with all her heart but she never really got closure from her first love Jason.

As she plugged in her iPod one of her favorite songs came on by a local artist and friend of hers. HOMEYHILL as the lyrics blared through the speakers it spoke to her " Fuck with me before it's too late". She laughed because it was way to late for Jason and he'd find that out really soon. As she drove home she rolled the windows down and let the cool air in as she prepared to talk to Dean.

When LT got home Dean was already home sitting on the couch he looked exhausted with all the paper work in front of him. She gave him his BROWN BETTY. This instantly got him up he loved Guyanese food. He remembered when LT made him chow mein for the first time.

As she seasoned the noodles and mixed vegetables with the Chinese sauce Dean was amazed when he saw how easy it was to make something so delicious. Naturally she had to share with him her favorite spot which was BROWN BETTY. LT hated to see Dean like this all caught up in a case. So she decided tonight would be all about him.

As he ate his chicken fried rice she walked to the bathroom and ran a bubble bath for him, she lit candles and turned On the radio. Once Dean heard the music she was playing he knew what she was doing. His lady always knew how to help him clear his head. As he finished putting away his paper work he made his way to the bathroom. LT stood there in a soft pink bathrobe with her hair wrapped with a few bobby pins in it.

Dean walked over to her and kissed her forehead. He slipped out of his work clothes and slid into the tub. "Your joining me aren't you?" He asked LT anticipating her answer. LT stood there with a sly smile and simply stated "of course, but we both know this won't just be a bath Dean". He smiled devilishly because she was right. LT slid into the tub and sat on top of Dean so they were face to face.

They just stared at one another for about ten seconds, not saying a word but knowing exactly what the other was thinking. Dean made the first move and kissed her passionately. As he slid inside her slowly LT began riding him while the water made small waves in there aria muse acrylic bath tub. That night they made love and got lost in one another.

THE DINNER

When LT arrived at the restaurant in her fitted blue suede dress with the back cut out and black pumps with a blue suede clutch to match she instantly regretted it because she forgot to mention it to Dean. She knew nothing would take place with Jason but it was in the back of her mind just how this would look to Dean. When she was seated Jason was already there with a drink in front of him.

"LT I ordered your favorite drink an amaretto sour, I remember how much you liked them". Jason said with a smile plastered on his face like he just won a noble peace prize. LT sat down and got right to it. "Jason what is this about you wouldn't let up so I'm here please say what you have to say so I can get home". LT said with dismay.

"Well damn Latanya, I thought two old friends could grab a bite to eat and catch up on what's been going on in one another's lives since we last saw one another, I see you're in a rush". He said. LT couldn't take the dog and pony show Jason was putting on and laid into him. "Listen Jason, I'm happier than I've ever been when we were together you were all I knew I always wanted to make YOU happy and by doing that I almost lost myself, I thought I could never love someone else after you hurt me on countless occasions but then Dean came along and now I see what a real man is and I wouldn't trade him for the world."

LT gushed while thinking about Dean. Jason sat at the table in shock like he couldn't believe what was coming out of her mouth. Jason recalled the relationship in a whole different way. "LT I'm going to be honest with you we were young, we only knew one another, as a man I needed more you were inexperienced I wanted to do things sexually that you just didn't want to explore." Jason tried

38

to explain. As the two sat in silence the waiter came back right in the nick of time. "What can I get the lovely couple this evening?".

The young waiter asked not knowing what he just interrupted. The two burst into laughter so loud that Jason had to grab LT's hand to calm her down. "I'll have the barbecue chicken with string beans and sweet potatoes" LT ordered. Jason took the same thing. "Jason what is this about really how much catching up do we really need we didn't end things on the best note." LT said Sternly now the irritation was kicking in.

"Well since you won't even wait for the food to get here I'll just say it, I'm getting married in the spring and I wanted you to hear it from me". Jason stated. LT spit her drink out as she heard what her ex lover was saying to her. The same man that couldn't come home without a lipstick stain on his collar or a number in his pocket just told her he'd be getting married in the spring. "Whose the lucky woman?" I really need to know LT stated eagerly. "I think you may know her Latanya her name is Jade Parrish". When I told her who you were she explained you to a tee she said you two went to junior high together." Jason said.

LT couldn't believe what she was hearing. The first girl she ever fought in America was marrying her first love all she could do was call for the waiter to bring another amaretto. "Well this I have to hear" LT exclaimed. "I met her at an art show my job sent me to take pictures , she was one of the artist there we clicked right away. Her piece was of a woman with no makeup, no weave, just all natural it kind of looked like you LT."

She couldn't believe what she was hearing the thing that made her and Jade have a brawl when they were younger is what inspired a piece of her artwork. That also brought her ex and archenemy together. "This isn't real, I can't believe what I'm hearing". LT just sat there in utter shock. Not wanting to hear anymore but couldn't help but sit there and listen. Jason led with "It happened when you finally decided to leave me officially Latanya. I knew I was wrong to

39

you on so many levels, it's like you were so good to me but I was young and dumb.

Losing you was the worse day of my life it left a void an empty hole I couldn't fill. I couldn't eat or sleep it started affecting my work. I had no one to talk to all the guys basically told me the day would come so how could I be surprised. My mom told me to leave you alone because she spoke with you and realized I wasn't right for you. Then Jade came along she was like a light at the end of a dark tunnel. We actually officially hooked up through some mutual friends we were at a concert and one thing led to another now we're getting married".

LT finally gathered her thoughts. This is what she'd wanted to hear since the day she decided to leave Jason. It was like a breath of fresh air. "Well Jay I wish you would've told me it was ANYONE else on the planet besides Jade but if you two are happy I can't be that mad, maybe she's grown up a bit from when we last exchanged words and fist, but nonetheless I'm happy you realized the errors of your ways and your man enough to admit you lost the best thing to happen to you". She said with a big smile on her face.

They both laughed and continued talking and catching up like the old friends they once were. Nalini sat at the bar looking at the whole exchange between LT and the stranger. She just thought about how much Jessica idolized Dean and LT. She couldn't understand why LT would jeopardize losing such a good man. She contemplated on walking over but she didn't want to overstep it could be nothing.

So she just decided to text her girlfriend and see what was going on. She'd only met LT a couple of times and she had no reason to think she was interested in anyone but Dean the way the two were around one another, so this was actually a surprise.

*Hey, Babe I'm at Soco with some friends and I see your partners girl here on a date, is everything okay with those two. hit me back *

She ended the text waiting for a response. She made sure to keep an eye on the two, because it's nothing worse than giving false news. Meanwhile at the table Jason was swooning over his fiancé Jade. "She's a great woman LT". He said matter-of-factly.

LT wasn't buying it but she kept a straight face as he told her more about the relationship. As much as I love Jade I can't lie in the back of my mind I can't help but think what if things didn't go down like that between us." He looked LT dead in her face to make sure she knew he wasn't pulling her leg. He went on... "my mother didn't get over you she told me it's something about Jade she can't put her finger on it, but she's not really for this marriage either...but then again no one could live up to you."

You're the greatest woman I know and my mom loves you what more can a man ask for. The two most important women in his life actually getting along and what did I do screw all it up. "Literally" LT interjected without even realizing she was thinking out loud he looked at her like a deer caught in the headlights.

He then moved closer and held her hands as he said. "LaTanya if you told me right now that you'd take me back I'd end things in a heartbeat." She sat there in the moment just still not believing that the words she'd always wanted to hear from Jason were finally being said.

But it was just to late the heartbreak he caused led her to the man she was meant to be with. Dean McKenner at that moment she realized they were still holding hands she took her hands out of his and cleared her throat so she didn't have to repeat herself. "Jason I've waited so long for you to say these things to me, but I want you to hear me when I tell you it is never going to happen. I have NEVER been more happy and satisfied in my life.

Dean is the only man for me. If you loved Jade as much as you say you do you would never disrespect her or your engagement like your doing right now... I now see you will never change. This is who you are and who you will always be a no good dog of a man.

Thank you for dinner". She said while getting up to leave. This was the last time the two would ever share a meal or the presence of one another it was finally over. As she made her exit she didn't even notice Nalini sitting there at the bar watching her every move.

PERMISSION

It was a warm spring day in Westfield, New Jersey. As Dean pulled up to the beautiful home on 344 Livingston Avenue he saw a familiar face out front planting flowers. He parked his CLA 250 in the driveway. As he made his way over to the beautiful woman he couldn't help but feel giddy inside. "Hey mrs. Defreitas you need some help". Dean said. As Lucinda turned around smiling she told Dean. "As a matter of fact I do, please run to the garage and bring two bags of soil please and thank you.

Dean got right to it. When he came back Lucinda was standing there admiring her bellflowers and chrysanthemums. Dean still smiling from ear to ear asked Lucinda if her husband was home as well. "Why yes he is Dean, something has you very excited you can't stop smiling." She said inquisitively. Dean just motioned for her to come in the house because he couldn't hold his excitement.

When the two got into the house Mr. Defreitas was sitting in the den reading a James Patterson novel. He loved a good murder mystery. He was shocked to see Dean way out in the country. That's what him and LT called New Jersey. "Well, well hey son what brings you to this side of the river?" Linden said while making his way over to Dean and gave the young man a firm handshake.

Dean was about to start pleading his case on why he wanted to marry their wonderful daughter but was interrupted by Lucinda asking if the men wanted some sorrel or ginger beer. " I'll have some water please." Dean was sweating profusely at this moment.

When Lucinda returned with drinks for everyone Dean began. "Latanya and I have been dating for several years now, I think about her before I go to sleep and she's the first thing I think about when I wake up. I say that to say I can't see myself with anyone else. She's my soulmate I honestly can't see myself with anyone else in this world. Linden smiled because he actually liked Dean. He knew exactly how LT felt about him. This was no surprise to him.

Lucinda on the other hand had her reservations. She told Dean his job scared her. "I don't want my daughter to be a widow. The way this world is going son any day can be your last." She continued. "Do you really think this is the right time for you two to wed?" Dean was so confused he didn't know where this was coming from he thought Linden would've been the one denying him his daughter not the woman he grew to adore.

"With all due respect Mrs. Defreitas I can't think of a better time to marry the woman of my dreams. You have raised a fine woman and I know she is the one for me. Whether we get married today, tomorrow or the next ten years Latanya will be my wife". Dean said firmly.

Linden let out a hearty laugh. The other two occupants in the room saw no humor in the topic at hand. He then proceeded to say "Dean yuh know yuh good I've been married to this woman almost thirty five years and I never stand up to she suh. Lucinda if I had to choose any man to take care of and marry my daughter it would be Mr. Dean Mckenner". He concluded.

Lucinda thought Linden would stand up for her but he didn't. She still had her reservations but she saw this was one battle she wouldn't win so she gave her blessings to her soon to be son in law. Dean beamed with happiness he was a thousand percent sure it would be Mr. Defreitas who'd be the one who would fight him on this decision to marry his daughter. He never thought Lucinda would take the news the way she did.

The three of them made there way to the dining room where Lucinda brought her famous cook up rice. LT had nothing on her mother's cooking Dean wanted to leave but he smelled the aroma and couldn't resist. Lucinda seemed to be coming around she had many questions for Dean. "so have you thought of a venue, when do you want to get married, when will you two have children. Dean almost choked on the last question. He just wanted to marry LT for now. Children seemed so distant until Lucinda brought the subject up.

"I'm ready whenever LaTanya is." Dean answered all the questions that were being thrown at him. Linden smiled and said "good answer son". The three laughed and continued to have lunch. When Dean was ready to leave he asked LT's parents to keep this visit a secret he wanted the proposal to be a surprise. She thought Dean was working. That's what he texted her when he arrived in New Jersey.

The Defreitas' had no problem keeping this between them and Dean. They realized how good he was for LT. They were there to pick up the pieces after Jason left her broken. When Latanya came to visit her parents crying her mom wanted to kill Jason. "I knew from day one I didn't like da damn bai" Lucinda said while trying to console her daughter. Her father took the more calmer approach. "listen baby, this is a minor set back the right one guh come along I just know it. When he does you're going to forget all about that blasted fool Jason." Linden told her while wiping her tears.

LT got herself together and through herself into her work legal and illegal. So when she met Dean Mckenner he was the breath of fresh air she'd been waiting for. As Dean drove back to the city Z100 played a song he couldn't help but blast. Jason derulo • MARRY ME•. If that wasn't a clear sign he was doing the right thing he didn't know what to believe. He now had to plan out the best proposal ever.

The next day he contacted his three sisters to tell them what was he was planning. They all were so happy for there brother. Cynthia had so many ideas she was an event planner in conyers, Georgia. Dean knew she'd be the most excited. That she was, she couldn't believe Dean finally decided to take the big step to settle down and marry the woman he loved. "Cyn, I know you have the whole wedding planned sis. I haven't even planned a proposal yet I wanted your insight and opinion. Dean asked his sister on his Bluetooth speaker through the car.

"Dean to say I've been waiting for this day would be an understatement. I knew once you introduced us to Latanya she was the one. The glow on your face, the love in your eyes I've never seen you have before. Little brother I've known for quite some time now. I was just waiting for this call." Cyn said beaming on the other line. Dean smiled just knowing he was making the right decision. Nothing ever felt so right in his life before this moment.

Since everyone was on board. It was time to prepare for the proposal. Dean was nervous and excited at the same time. He'd never felt this way before. He had girlfriends before and the occasional fling. But Latanya changed his whole perspective. She was his other half. His one true love. Cyn told him LT deserved an over-the-top proposal, just for putting up with him. Dean got a kick out of that one.

Dean decided the next weekend he'd take LT to a cabin on the outskirts of New York. His parents owned it. He would put candles and rose petals all over the place and cook LT a chef Gordon Ramsay special. The roasted beef filet is what he decided on. He wanted the night to be perfect so he asked captain Casey for the weekend off. Dean was a cop for over ten years and never took time off. Casey needed to know what actually made the work robot take a whole weekend off.

"She's really the one, isn't she Dean?" Casey said with a smile on his face. "Cap. I don't even know how to put into words how this woman makes me feel." Dean said while thinking about LT. Casey was proud of him all of the things Dean went through in his entire life he definitely deserved a win.

He was long overdue. Casey knew just by looking at Dean that he'd found a good one. He was proud of Dean. Casey was old school he didn't believe in shacking up. He always told Dean LT would make him an honest man. The way he'd see Dean daydream at his desk or come to work smiling ear to ear he was waiting for this day. He was glad to witness it. Young black love at its finest.

THE BACKLASH

As Jessica sat at her desk reading the text from Nalini she was in disbelief. She felt like there was more to the story or at least hoped it was more. For now she had to figure out how to approach Dean. When Dean came back to his desk Jessica decide to go with a subtle approach. "So partner how are things with you and LT going?" Jessica questioned. Dean lit up and replied. "Wonderful I love her more and more each day." Jessica was even more nervous now to tell Dean about the message she just received from her girlfriend.

"Do you know where LT is right now Dean?" She continued her interrogation. Dean looked at his partner puzzled and confused. "I'm not sure, is there a reason for these questions jess. Just spill it what's going on?" He asked. "Listen I don't want to cause a rift between you and Latanya but Nalini just texted me saying LT is on a date with a light skinned man. She didn't know if you two were still together or not." Jessica said not knowing what to expect.

Dean's dark smooth face instantly turned red. He wasn't sure what Nalini thought she saw but it couldn't be LT, Could it? As he sat at his desk trying to put it all together one person came to mind Jason her ex. But why and how long had she been going on secret dates with the man she said hurt her beyond repair. Dean was fuming he slammed his fist on the desk so hard it startled everyone in the bullpen.

"Dean calm down." Ramirez got up and put her arm on his shoulder. "Remember where you are right now. I'm sure there is an explanation for this I've never seen anyone look at someone the way Latanya looks at you. Take a minute regroup and come back. She insisted. As Dean got up to take that walk captain Casey called them both into his office. He heard the commotion and brought them into his office. "What's going on, is there a reason you're breaking up official NYPD property Mckenner??" Casey asked.

"Dean is fine captain he just got a little hot over the case". Ramirez tried to cover it up. Casey was an old timer he knew when women trouble was affecting a man he was married three times. He finally got it right on the third try. "Dean I think you need to take a few days off. I can't have you losing it in front of these rookies". Casey told Dean.

He hadn't realized how much of a show he'd actually put on. "But cap. What about the caymans." Dean pleaded. "Monroe will most likely still be around, I can't have you out of it trying to bring someone down". Casey told him. The talk with Casey really brought him back to reality. "You're right cap. I don't know what came over me. I'm going to head home now." Dean said as he walked out of the precinct.

As Dean drove home all he could think about was LT with another man. He wasn't even mad she was out with someone else. What made his blood boil is the fact she kept it from him. He couldn't go home just yet he made a stop at a local bar. He needed to take the edge off. First the case now this it was just to much. He went into VIBES right off the van Wyck and Liberty. The place wasn't as packed as it usually was on a Friday night. He ordered a Johnny walker Black with coke. He just sat there fuming his fourth drink in he realized it was enough.

Dean got up and staggered the bartender told him have a seat he'd call a cab. He saw Deans badge and knew how hard it was out here for black men and even more so a black cop. Plus he didn't want any blow back on the bar. As Dean got into the cab he thanked the bartender. He made sure he tipped him handsomely. When Dean pulled up to the apartment he shared with LT he realized it was time to face the music.

He made his way into the apartment stumbling and knocking everything over. Smooth Mckenner he thought to himself. LT walked out the room and asked if he was ok. She knew he was supposed to be at work so that was the first question she asked.

"Aren't you supposed to be at work hun?" She asked while holding Dean up. He replied "we've both been places we don't belong today huh hun." He stated with disdain. LT had already forgotten about the dinner with Jason. She felt like that chapter was finally closed. Little did she know Jason wasn't that easy to get rid of.

"Dean what are you talking about? Why are you drunk and not at work?." She was genuinely confused at this point. "So you were on a date today with whom? Whose the mystery man Latanya. Dean interrogated her. LT was confused how he knew, she wasn't going to keep it from him it really did slip her mind. Dean was staggering all through the apartment at this point. He was looking for the Johnny walker he kept in the apartment. LT needed to get him seated to try to explain what happened.

"Dean, baby listen to me. Nothing happened I had dinner with Jason he told me he's getting married is all. It slipped my mind you've had a lot on your mind I wasn't trying to keep it from you." Dean gave her a look she'd never seen in his eyes before. He was so angry he got up and punched a medium sized hole in the wall.

She'd never seen him this angry. It was all new to her. He began with " Of all the men to have dinner with and not tell me about it Latanya HIM!. He said referring to Jason. I hate him the things he did to you broke you it took me forever to break through your walls. Then here you go the first chance you get you're right back in his arms." Dean said not really meaning it but his ego and pride were hurt.

LT stood there in disbelief. She couldn't believe what she was hearing. The man she loved telling her she would go back to the man that made her feel like love was a lie. I'm going to go Dean because you aren't yourself right now. So before you say anything else that you're going to regret I'm going to leave. She left her drunk detective on the couch and packed an overnight bag. LT was so hurt. When she texted Ariel the details she felt the tears rolling down her face.

When she arrived at Ariel's home Lane opened the door to a teary eyed Latanya. "Hey sis. What's going on I knew you were on your way over but Ariel didn't tell me it was an issue come in". Lane said as LT made it into the vestibule Ariel came down the stairs of there two story home. She told Lane she would take over from here. As Ariel consoled LT she needed a better understanding of what really took place.

When LT did a run through of the events Ariel sat quietly. She knew Dean was wrong for what was said but she had to let LT know what she did was wrong as well. She didn't believe in bashing men. Dean was entitled to how he felt but what was said was overboard.

"Listen Latanya he was wrong and right." That's how Ariel started her advice hear me out she continued. "Dean loves you unconditionally anyone who knows the two of you knows that. Why would you keep that from him?" Ariel really wanted to know. LT really didn't have an explanation. In all actuality she felt like she wanted to close the chapter with Jason. She thought when she told Dean they would just have a good laugh over the foolishness Jason tried to pull. This was in no shape or form how she thought things would go.

"Sis you can stay in the guest room for as long as you like, but I know you two will get through this because what you guys have is unbreakable." Ariel concluded "thanks Ari. I don't know where I would be without you. He just needs to cool off but I have to work in the morning I'm going to the caymans I didn't even get to let him know because of this stupid fight." LT explained. As the two hugged LT couldn't thank Ariel enough for being a listening ear and the advisor of her life.

The next morning Dean woke up with a pounding headache and a mean hangover. He was searching for LT. He had no idea when he even got home. When he woke up to the text message from LT he was confused.

I don't know what came over you last night, what you said was out of line. I know I was wrong for what I did but I didn't cheat on you I'd never do that. The fact that you even insinuated that I would, hurt me. I'll be in the Cayman Islands for a few days we can talk when I get back.

He knew something happened but the extent of this message he received he knew he must've said something stupid. But what was it. He hopped in the shower and got himself together. He knew one person that would know exactly what happened. When Dean showed up to Ariels home she just shook her head.

They embraced one another and Dean went inside with her. "Ariel how is baby girl doing?" He began trying to win her over. "She's fine getting bigger by the day." Ariel answered. "good I'm glad to hear that" he said. Ariel jumped right in after that. "Dean LT knew she was wrong for what she did but you took it a little to far".

The puzzled look on Deans face said it all. He had no clue what was said. "Dean you told LT she ran back to Jason and basically told her she was cheating on you what the hell came over you?" She explained to him. Dean was disgusted with himself. He would never say something like that to LT if he was sober. He was angry he had to admit but that was a line they'd never crossed with one another.

"Ariel I was out of it. The fact I had to hear about the meeting or date or whatever it was from my partner just threw me for a loop. I never wanted it to get this bad. I'm actually going to propose to LT." Dean said not realizing he forgot to tell Ariel. She cut him off instantly. "Wait what? when? how? Where? He'd known her for as long as he knew Latanya so he knew Ariel was planning the wedding already. But for now he had to get his girl back.

CAYMANS

When LT arrived in the Cayman Islands she couldn't even wrap her head around what had taken place between her and Dean. She'd never seen him behave like that before. They had arguments in the past but this was over the top. She just kept replaying what he said to her over and over. She knew he couldn't have meant it. But just knowing it's something that was on his mind made her wonder.

She knew she could never go back to Jason. That wasn't even a thought. This fight was uncalled for. She received so many text messages from Dean apologizing but she needed time to cool off as well. She came for business but she decided to make it a little personal. LT loved flowers and the Caymans were known for the flora and fauna at the botanical garden.

She needed me time. She didn't want to worry about the outside world. As she walked through she saw a familiar face her friend from college Erin. She walked behind her and said " so they're letting party crashers in the country now?" Erin hadn't seen LT in years but she couldn't forget her college roommate.

She turned around with a huge smile on her face. Her chipmunk cheeks instantly turned red. She resmbled LT they were always mistaken for sisters. As the two women embraced one another they both felt excitement. Erin adored LT they met on their first day of college. Both fresh out of high school ready to take on the world. When LT walked up to administration she thought she had everything she needed. But she'd left one thing in her dads car her ID.

The woman at the desk joked with her and said "so you brought everything but the kitchen sink huh?". They both laughed. Then as she turned around to call her dad he was walking into the building. "oh my god thank you so much daddy I didn't want you to have to drive all the way back here." LT said to her father. "Listen baby girl I'd drive to the Himalayan mountains for you." Linden explained. LT just smiled from ear to ear she just loved her father so much.

When she was finally done with registration and got to her dorm someone was already at there. She had two posters up on the wall one of Bob Marley and the other was Marilyn Monroe. When LT walked in Erin was startled but then went right in for a hug. LT was a little confused. "Well aren't you friendly" LT stated. Erin just smiled and said I'm from the south honey this is how we say hello". Erin told her. The two just laughed. " where are you from, miss lady". Erin questioned LT. "Well I'm originally from Guyana but I've lived in Jamaica, Queens most of my life, now I'll be here in Sullivan county for school". LT answered. The two knew instantly they would get along.

They were both in the same nursing program at school. The two ended up becoming great friends. Nowhere on campus did you see one without the other. LT had decided during her second year that she really wasn't interested in becoming a nurse so she switched majors. They still hung out but Erin's schedule was a little less Lenient. LT had lost her partner in crime. That was just the beginning of there friendship drifting.

When Erin was done studying and cramming for exams she was exhausted. So the friends really didn't have much time for one another. When graduation came around they celebrated together but parted ways. So this reunion was long overdue. Erin just stood there staring at LT in awe she really stayed fit and filled out since college. Erin had a medium build. She was slim but had baby making hips. She got it from her momma. It must've been her southern roots. The two women just kept complimenting one another until they finally decided on drinks.

Erin was gushing over here boyfriend Mario who had brought her to the Caymans for there nine month anniversary. He was busy with some business so he would meet up with them afterwards. While Erin told her about all that she had missed while they were busy living their lives LTs thoughts drifted to Dean. "Hello Latanya I've been rambling on for like twenty minutes, what's going on with you how is Jason?" Erin asked.

That snapped LT back to reality. "I'm sorry about that I have a lot on my mind. But Jason isn't it. We broke up four years ago. He was a dog girl." LT exclaimed. Erin just gave her the side eye. She'd been telling LT through college leave that no good man alone. "Well tell me about the new guy that has all your attention then." Erin questioned. "Dean, where do I begin he is the epitome of a great man. I love him so much although we aren't on great terms right now. When I get home we will make things right. As soon as she was about to get into the story Mario walked in.

"Hello ladies I hope I'm not interrupting." He said when LT turned around to meet the mysterious voice she was taken aback. He was so handsome he looked just like Antonio sabato Jr dimples included. She felt like she knew his face but couldn't place him.

"Babe this is my college roommate Latanya." Erin said. As the two shook hands Mario couldn't help but admire the beauty that stood in front of him. Erin saw the look the two gave one another. So she continued with "Latanya was just telling me about her boyfriend Dean." Erin knew she didn't have to worry about LT being interested in Mario but he had a wondering eye. This was a makeup vacation. She found messages between him and three other women.

LT noticed what Erin was doing so she just said "it's a long story, but we are working through some things." Lucinda had taught LT to never discuss your love life with people you're not close to. That leaves a door open for anything. Just sitting there looking at Mario and Erin made her miss Dean even more. "So Latanya what's your plans? How long will you be here in the Caymans?"

Mario questioned her. "Two more nights." She answered. "We are going to a friend of mines party tomorrow night. Drinks and dancing. We'd love for you to come." He added. LT couldn't remember the last time she actually went out so she decided to unwind.

"I have some errands in the morning, but I'll call Erin and get the details." She said while making her exit. When LT was gone out of the restaurant Mario questioned Erin about her. "So where do you know her from? I've never seen you two together." She explained they were playing catch up and that was her college roommate. Erin thought Mario was interested in LT so she was hesitant to say more.

The reality of it was LT was Mario's biggest competitor in the gold business. He'd heard of the beautiful batterer they called LT. He never imagined that she would look like that . Nonetheless she was a threat to his business. He'd find out as much about her as possible. So he ordered another round. That always got his girl talking and loose. The one bad trait Erin had she couldn't control her liquor. So she started telling Mario everything she knew about LT he planned on using this to his advantage.

The next night they all met at the most popular lounge in the Caymans THE FLAMINGO. LT wore a short jumpsuit. It had gold sequins and showed off her curves. She just came for the vibes. She was ready to go home and make up with Dean. When Mario saw her walk in he called over his partner Jose to let him know she'd arrived. They were LT's competition from Venezuela. It's always been a war between Guyana and Venezuela. If it wasn't the gold it was the oil. This was finally time to settle the score.

When LT finally made it over to the section everyone had their eyes on her. She was a force to be reckoned with. All those workouts showed. When she sat down she felt an awkward vibe from Jose. Although Erin told her that's just how he was she knew something was off. When she had a chance to step away she called

Dean. She needed to hear his voice. The two usually spoke every night this was their worse fight ever.

"Hi, how are you?" He said sounding defeated. LT felt the hurt in his voice but she felt like she had to be strong. She never wanted to treat him this way but what he said was still eating away at her. "Hey I'm fine just wanted to check in, I really miss you but I needed you to cool down and I got a shift I didn't get to tell you about I'm sorry for that." She said trying to sound nonchalant. Dean could tell she missed him but was being the stubborn woman he loved so much. "LT are you coming back to the section?" A female voice said in the background. She forgot where she was for a moment. Dean just told her to get back to whatever it was She was doing she deserved to enjoy herself. In all reality she just wanted to be home with Dean.

When she got back to the section the men asked her if she was ok. LT was ready to go now but Mario wanted to see if she was who he thought she was. He went straight for the kill. "How's Monroe LT." Her face got serious when she heard the question. No one outside of her business had knowledge of Monroe. She tried to play it off but her face gave it away. "That's who you were talking to over there wasn't it?" He continued to question. "I'm not sure who you think I am but you have me mistaken for someone else". she said.

She didn't know what to do or who Mario really was but she had to get in contact with Monroe and fast. She told them she was going to the restroom after the uncomfortable run in and snuck out the club. She called Monroe when she got back to hotel. "Monroe I'm sorry to call you so late but we may have been compromised." LT explained the situation to Monroe. When she was finished Monroe told her Mario was their biggest competition. LT didn't know what to say when Monroe was done telling her what Mario was capable of. She knew she had to get out of the caymans and fast.

Her flight was at six am the next day but she was on high alert. LT always had protection on her. She knew the business she was in could lead to something like this. It was a smooth ride up until now. She was prepared for anything that came her way. The next morning she got out of the Caymans safe and sound hoping that was the last she would hear from Mario but something in her gut said this was just the beginning.

THE PROPOSAL

As Dean and Lane walked into Zales the jewelry store Lane started laughing. Dean stood there confused. "What's funny bro?" Dean asked puzzled. Lane just kept laughing then finally said "I can't believe you almost ruined something great." He heard the story and had to poke a little fun at his friend. "Of all the things to say to a woman." He continued but Dean wasn't trying to hear it, today was going to be a good day he could feel it. "I had a lot going on I took it to far, but LT knows how I feel about her. I'm here aren't I she's going to be my wife." Dean said.

"If she says yes." Lane said mockingly. The two laughed and went to the engagement rings section. It took ten minutes for Dean to find the one he knew LT would love. A precious bride cushion-cut blue sapphire ring. It was 14k white gold. He knew LT didn't care to much for yellow gold. This was the one he just knew it. Lane was impressed it was a good choice. Lane sent a picture to Ariel to make sure it was just right. The amount of heart emojis she sent let them know that ring was the one.

Ariel was back at the apartment setting it up for the arrival of LT. She had lavender candles lit all over the place. She found platycodons to sprinkle all over the apartment LT loved the purple flowers. She was so excited for her friend. She even made them a dinner to celebrate. She made stuffed salmon with wild rice pilaf with sautéed butternut squash.

She could throw down when she wanted to. This was just one of her talents that kept Lane happy. When Lane and Dean got back to the apartment they knew it would look nothing like how they left it but Ariel outdid herself. "She might marry you instead" Dean joked as he walked through the door. Lane laughed at the corny joke. "Babe this is absolutely amazing" Lane said while leaning in for a kiss. "Thank you guys, this is my girl we're talking about I wasn't about to have it looking anyhow, I hooked it up." Ariel boasted. She definitely did they couldn't even deny it.

"As much as I appreciate what the two of you have done for LT and I, I need you both gone before my soon to be fiancé comes home thank you." Dean said with a sly smile across his face. Ariel was disappointed but she understood why he had to do it alone. "Fine but make sure LT calls me as soon as you're done proposing bro." Ariel whined. Lane just laughed and told her "let's go babe, you have a whole wedding to plan with Deans sister. You will be ok."

When they finally left the apartment Dean took a shower and prepared what he was going to say to the love of his life when she arrived. He made sure to get a fresh shape up and new cologne.

Dean went as far as to buy a suit for the occasion. He wanted LT to know how much she meant to him. He lit all the lavender candles Ariel left around the apartment he had fifteen minutes to get himself fully together before LT got in. He made sure to tell her to change her clothes. He texted her he was taking her out to dinner this made the surprise even better.

He knew LT loved to eat and she always took extra outfits with her when she traveled. He was so nervous he didn't remember ever being this nervous about anything in his life. When he heard the key turning in the front door he fixed himself one last time. He even checked his breath one last time. When LT finally walked in she didn't know what was going on the apartment looked beautiful and there was Dean standing there in a suit. She thought this was his way of apologizing for how he behaved so the proposal was still a surprise.

"Hey babe welcome home I missed you so much." Dean said in a sultry tone LT was still confused as to why every candle was lit and Dean had a suit on. All of the signs were in her face and she still didn't get it. "Dean I get it you're sorry. I am too that was wrong of me not telling you about the dinner with Jason but nothing happened." She pleaded. Dean just stood there with a big grin on his face. "Let me get your jacket babe." He said softly. LT just stood there confused as all hell. When Dean finally got her coat off and saw her outfit he was in awe of his beautiful fiancé to be. LT stood there in her burgundy lace dress with a long slit down her side. She was prepared for a dinner date with Dean. When she turned around Dean was on one knee with the most beautiful ring she'd ever seen. She was at a loss for words. Dean started off with kissing her on her hand then said " Latanya ever since I saw you that first day at the airport I knew you were the woman I'd spend the rest of my life with. I never knew I could feel this way about another human. To say you complete me would be an understatement. You are and always will be my other half through this life and the next."

He continued with the famous line "will you give me the honor of being my wife?" LT stood there in shock not really registering what was happening. Dean took her hand and asked again "will you marry me?" She finally snapped out of the trance she was in and said "yes Dean Mckenner. Yes to forever with you I love you." He put the beautiful ring on her and kissed her. "This isn't the apology I expected" she said laughing while tears rolled down her face. She didn't expect a proposal at all. This was the best surprise ever.

She loved Dean so much. She didn't think there was a life after Jason boy was she wrong. Although the threat of Mario loomed over her she still said yes. She didn't let that stop her happiness she would live in the now. Monroe told her to take a break until they got the full details on what Mario knew about there operation. What a perfect distraction the man she loved proposing to her. She couldn't wait to call Ariel after dinner.

"Oh my god you were in on it?. I thought you were my girl". LT said to Ariel over FaceTime. Ariel and Lane both had there faces in the screen at this time just smiling from ear to ear. "We both knew sis. We had to keep this one secret, no more secrets though". Lane said. That one hit LT like a ton of bricks she'd kept a secret from them all. The fact that it was becoming a little dangerous finally put her life into perspective. She knew she'd one day have to make a choice. Dean or the empire she would one day take over. But for now she would enjoy her engagement. She had time to think about where her life would take her another day.

THE WEDDING

Dean didn't want to wait to marry LT he was ready since he proposed. Cyn was already working on a venue. Ariel was doing the catering and flowers everyone played there part. When LT went to tell her parents they were both genuinely happy for her. Her dad even told her how Dean shut her mother down and was determined to marry her they all had a good laugh off of that one. "Lt yuh sure dis da man ya wan be wid" Lucinda asked when it was just the two of them. Dean and Linden were having Johnny walker and cokes on the porch.

"Mom I love him. I feel for him what I never felt with Jason. He makes me feel safe and loved. I never had to worry about him cheating or hurting me the way I've been hurt" she tried to explain to her mother. Lucinda just sat there and listened to her daughter. LT continued. "The way you are with daddy I'm ready for that, that real love." Lucinda understood now how her daughter was feeling. She was not the young teen they brought from Guyana. She was an adult and it was time for her to respect it and let her make decisions for herself.

Lucinda stayed quiet for a few seconds realizing she really couldn't stop this union. "Latanya if you believe this is who you're meant to be with I won't stand in your way. I want nothing but the best for you. Whatever your decision is I stand behind it. I wan wah is Bess fa yuh." Lucinda's accent always came out when she didn't get her way. But she knew LT wasn't changing her mind and Dean made it very clear when he asked for her hand in marriage that he was here to stay.

"Who da tell him about you and Jason dinner?" Lucinda questioned. She was very inquisitive or nosey when it came to LT. "Mom his coworkers girlfriend saw us and thought I was on a date. She told Jessica it was one big misunderstanding." LT told her mother who had an annoyed look on her face. "People don't mind their own damn business eh." Lucinda said with disgust. LT just laughed and said "don't worry mom nothing can break the bond Dean and I have." Lucinda was old school she didn't grow up in the era when being gay was okay.

"Jessica apologized already we got past it ma" LT said trying to convince her mom to drop it. Once Lucinda started it wouldn't end. Dean walked in right in time to save LT from a lecture. "Babe your old man and I are going to watch the game, the knicks are playing we'll be here awhile" Dean said seeing LT's face made him laugh. He knew her mother was getting on her nerves. LT thought they were on there way out but nope she had more time with her mom now. "Mom can we talk about the wedding please." LT whined. Her mother got the hint after that and dropped the issue.

LT decided to help her mom prepare dinner for the men. She told LT this will be her life now cooking, cleaning and babies. She knew what her mom was hinting. She was ready for a grand child but LT wanted to wait a couple more years when she was comfortable and actually ready. Everyone was on her back about having children. She wanted two children but the life she was living there was no room for a child. Then to think of bringing a child in the world kind of scared her.

Lucinda saw the look on LTs face and changed the subject. "Your father and I are going to pay for the wedding. It's tradition and I refuse to have you put a penny." She told her daughter. LT didn't feel like arguing she was actually relieved because no one would ask where she got money to pay for the lavish wedding she was going to have it all worked out. "Mom I saw my dream dress it's beautiful." LT said while smiling from ear to ear.

She went online and found the most beautiful trumpet mermaid V-neck court train wedding dress. She just knew it was the one she'd walk down the aisle to meet her forever in. She pulled her IPhone out with the pictures she saved on it. Her mother was in awe of how beautiful the dress was. " I'm going to the fitting baby". Lucinda said with a sly smile. "The mother of the bride must look good too." She added. LT couldn't help but laugh at her mom. It was going to be an event between her mother and maid of honor Ariel It would be great just what she needed to take her mind off the business.

When the night ended LT and Dean said goodnight to her parents and headed back to Queens. LT told him he left her to the wolf also known as her mom. "LT she isn't that bad". Dean tried to justify what he'd done. She wasn't trying to hear it. He took her hand in his while he gripped the steering wheel with his left hand and said. "Latanya I want you forever". LT couldn't help but blush her dark brown skin turned pink . Dean still gave her butterflies. When they got home they made love and slept the rest of the night away.

The next few weeks were hectic. The wedding was happening. Lucinda booked The Royal manor. It was going to be a summer wedding. The one Latanya always dreamed of having. She had her dress Ariel and Cyn helped her with the cake tasting and flowers her mom took care of everything else. Dean only had only job to show up and he got to pick out what his best man Lane would wear and his groomsmen. LT had the final say but she wanted him to feel like he was apart of her wedding.

The day finally arrived July eighteenth. The sun was out the birds chirped and Latanya looked absolutely stunning. Her mother and father looked at their baby girl and Lucinda couldn't help but cry. The day she'd dream of was actually happening. Her bridesmaids wore gold sequins dresses. They all looked beautiful Deans three sisters and Ariel. The groomsmen wore black tuxes and gold ties. When she finally made it to the end of the aisle Linden let his baby girl go after a long hug. She tried not to cry but a tear fell down her face. When she looked at Dean standing there with the biggest smile on his face she thought to herself "what did I do to get this lucky". Dean stood there in his Blue suit custom fitted to his fit physique.

LT couldn't stop staring at Dean it all felt like a dream. She snapped out of it when the pastor said "LT your vows please." She turned to Ariel who passed her a small piece of paper. She read her vows aloud meaning every word. "Dean I still remember you asking me to buy me a latte. Mr. 8C is what Ariel and I called you for months." Everyone laughed. She then continued. " you've help mold me into the woman I am today I want you to know I love you so much I love the way you make me feel and I want to grow old and gray with you." LT concluded. With tears streaming down her face now.

Dean just wiped her tears and whispered I love you before he read his vows. "Latanya I knew the day I walked up to you I'd marry you. I couldn't get you off my mind. No matter what I did there you were. Now as I stand here today I am ready to give you my all I want you to know my heart is yours. I want to spend the rest of my days with you." As he concluded there wasn't a dry eye in the room. When the pastor finally said you may kiss the bride it was an uproar everyone was excited.

The reception was everything LT imagined. She wanted a DJ and a live band. She got exactly that. The band sang all the old songs she grew up listening to while she and her mom cleaned the house on sunday mornings. Linden and LT did their father daughter dance to dance with my father by Luther Vandross. Then when it was time for their first dance as husband and wife Dean chose NE-YO's Stop this world from spinning. It was LTs favorite song of all time. She started crying all over again. When they finished the dj put on soca and LT's tears were gone. Her family gathered around her and they partied the night away.

THE HONEYMOON

As Dean and LT drove to the airport they couldn't stop giggling like two school children. They were on there way to the honeymoon LT planned for them. They were going to Maldives it was a long flight so they decided to fly with EMIRATES first class. They couldn't wait to get to their destination. Dean initiated everything LT was pouring champagne as Dean walked up behind her. As he started to kiss on her neck LT could feel every hair on her body rising. Dean just had a hold over her.

He turned her around and said to her " this will be my first time with a married woman". LT started laughing and told him he didn't have any sense. All his romance was out the window. He wanted her in every way possible. He kissed her passionately and took her over to the bed. He managed to grab some strawberries as well. He took off LT's clothes slowly. He wanted to see his wife's body. He stood over her staring in awe. Her body was craving his.

When Dean traced her body with the strawberry he then did the same with his tongue. This drove her wild. She'd never felt this way before. They'd made love before but it felt different this time. Dean made his way to that special spot that he now called his special place. As he tasted his wife for the first time LT let out a soft moan. Deans tongue was in and out of her it felt like pure ecstasy. She screamed forgetting they weren't home.

Dean stretched his hand up to cover her mouth. He was overwhelming her with pleasure. He finally came up for air. Latanya laid there still shaking from her orgasms. Dean smiled. He felt a sense of pride. Pleasing his wife was going to be his goal from this day forward. When she finally got her bearings together LT climbed on top of Dean. She made sure they were face to face while she slid him inside of her. She closed her eyes while she rode him. When she was about to climax she climb off of him and started performing oral.

As LT started to get into a rhythm the flight attendant came in to ask if everything was ok. She immediately turned back around. Dean and LT stopped momentarily to laugh. Then they both decided they should wait until they actually got to their honeymoon suite. They slept for the rest of the flight. When they arrived at ANANTARA the villa they were going to call home for the next week they were welcomed with two glasses of champagne. "I could get used to this Mrs. Mckenner." Dean said proudly LT just looked at him and smiled.

They finally made it to there room it was an over water pool villa. The scenery was immaculate. Neither of the two had ever seen anything like it in person. Dean wanted to go for a swim he hadn't taken a proper vacation in years. His cases always got in the way. This was his time. They made love in the shower and changed into swim wear. LT chose a pink two piece and Dean wore a pair of black swim trunks. They looked like models out of an ebony magazine.

They did a couple of laps then finally went to dinner. Dean let LT pick his outfit it matched hers. They both wore white. She picked out linen pants and a linen button up for him. She wore an all white crochet dress that showed her curves. When they got to dinner a complimentary bottle of champagne was waiting. "This is so amazing Latanya you really outdid yourself. See this is why I married you". Dean said jokingly. LT looked at him and said "I know it's not the only reason". while putting a strawberry in her mouth seductively. Dean could feel himself getting in the mood so he talked about something else.

"How's work babe, we are always so wrapped up in life I don't get to really ask you about it?" Dean asked. LT was actually at a loss for words. She hadn't thought about work or her gold business in the past two days. It actually felt good. " work is work honestly. I still enjoy travelling and seeing the world it was meant for me to be a flight attendant." She said while putting chicken in her mouth. Dean had a feeling something else was on her mind. He went into detective mode.

"Something is bothering you. What is it babe?" Dean questioned. LT couldn't tell him about Mario so she went with plan B. "Babe it's mom she's ready to be a grandmother. We had a talk the other day and she is pushing. Are you ready?" She asked Dean hoping he wasn't just yet. He surprised her and said "yes I am. I've been ready since the first day I met you. I knew you'd be the woman to have my children and take my last name. But if you're not ready I can wait." LT finally realized she had become a WE she was no longer Latanya Defreitas. She was now Latanya Mckenner. She was a married woman and all of her decisions from here on out would affect Dean.

"Babe I just want to enjoy us for now. I want to have your children and be a family. But maybe in another two years if that's ok." She said waiting on his response. "It's your body and your decision. When it's our time we will know. So for now I just want to enjoy you." Dean said. She breathed a sigh of relief. They went for a walk around the compound and looked at the sights. They truly did love one another. That undeniable love that neither one had ever felt before. They enjoyed the rest of their honeymoon not ready to go home and face the chaos that was coming.

THE THREAT

When LT and Dean got back to the apartment they received so many gifts. Dean figured most of it was stuff LT wanted so he went to take a nap. They got picture frames, aprons, gift cards and wine glasses. LT was about half way through when she noticed an envelope with a badge seal stamp. It had no return address. The initials were MG. She wasn't sure who it was from. When she opened it gold dust came out. The writing in the note was handwritten, It read:

> Congratulations mi amor. Sorry Erin and I didn't attend. I'm guessing our invites were lost in the mail. I would like to invite you to a meeting I'll be having in Venezuela. You're presence would be greatly appreciated. Until we meet again Mrs. Mckenner. Sincerely, MG.

LT felt a cold shiver down her spine. She was so confused she always felt like she covered herself. But Erin was always chatty so she probably told him everything she knew about LT. She went to the room to make sure Dean was still asleep. When she saw he was she went to the bathroom to call Monroe. When she got in the bathroom and made the call. Monroe picked up and said "what's wrong I told you to take some time". LT was a little frantic while telling Monroe what happened. Monroe told her to calm down and let her know he'd take care of it but she had to go to the meeting.

LT just didn't feel right about the whole situation. She had that gut feeling that something bad was coming. But she knew one day someone would come for her spot so it was time to boss up and show them who she really was. When she hung up with Monroe she burned the letter at the stove before bed. When she went into the room Dean was snoring. She just chuckled. The fact that she couldn't tell him what was going on started to take a toll on her. She knew she couldn't keep this double life up. In that moment she realized what she had to do.

It was time to become the wife and mother to his children. She was finally ready. The fact that they knew where she lived was enough of a threat for her to want to go straight. She had to figure out how she'd get to the meeting she had another two weeks off because she'd never taken a vacation. She loved working so much and she was always travelling so it never felt like she needed one. Dean was going back to work the following week so she would tell him she was visiting her family in Guyana. Since she had some time off.

The next day when she told Dean he was fine with it because he knew he'd be back at work. His cases were waiting for him anyway. He actually missed work just a bit. The detective In him was ready to get back in the field. The next week LT was walking on egg shells. She was anxious to hear what Mario wanted exactly.

She knew she was Monroe's best sales rep. As Monroe called her, but it was time she got out of the game. She'd made her decision it was time to wrap this life up and put it behind her. But it wasn't as easy as she was hoping.

When she arrived in Venezuela a car was waiting for her. The driver took her to a hotel in Macuto. The Olé caribe, if it was under different circumstances she would've enjoyed her stay. When she got to the front desk an envelope was given to her by the receptionist. It read :

Welcome, LT I hope you enjoyed your flight dinner will be at 7pm sharp. I hope to see you there. Wear something nice. See you then.

LT sucked her teeth and made her way to her room. She made sure to lock her door and move the couch to block the door. She didn't want anyone uninvited to come in. Monroe always told her to cover herself no matter what. She understood why those precautions where instilled in her today. She always felt like she was the only one doing her business. She'd forgotten about the competition. That was a mistake she wouldn't ever make again.

She wore one of her famous pants suits to the dinner meeting. This was after all business. When she got there it was just Mario and Jose. The same man she got the vibe from in the Cayman Islands. Mario welcomed her like she was the guest of honor. LT never felt more uncomfortable. But she had to stand her ground. "Why am I here Mario" she jumped right in. Mario laughed and asked Jose to step away. He saw how uneasy LT felt. He wanted her to feel a little more comfortable. When Jose got up he shot LT a look that she felt through her whole body.

"Well I want in on your little business. I know Monroe could always use a Venezuelan partner. We can help one another." Mario said with a smug look on his face. LT couldn't believe what she was hearing. "Why would Monroe want you in on his business you're doing well for yourself you don't want a partner you want the whole business." LT told him. "I've heard about all of your partnerships you've double crossed everyone. What makes this any different?" She asked wanting answers.

"I've had a change of heart the way Erin speaks about you I don't want to kill you and upset her" he said with a straight face. This took LT by surprise that her friend who she hadn't really spoken to in years was the reason she was alive right now. She kept a strong face and told him if he wanted to kill her he'd better do it right now, Because there was no way Monroe would ever have a partnership with such scum.

Mario admired LTs tenacious attitude. He'd heard she wasn't a push over. She stood firmly and wouldn't budge. "I see you're loyal. I wish I had more people in my circle like that" Mario said in a charming voice. This was actually a recruitment dinner. LT caught on when he told her about the loyalty. He told her he was looking to expand his business. Since she was good at what she did he wanted her on his team instead of Monroe's.

"As much as I appreciate the offer I'm not interested. My loyalty is with Monroe I can't help with whatever is going on in your organization. I wish you luck but you'll have to find someone else." LT said to him with a straight face. He couldn't do anything more at this point her mind was made up. "I understand this is why I wanted you but a man can only ask for so much." he said defeated.

LT felt a weight come off her shoulders when the dinner was over. She still had an uneasy feeling, like something terrible was coming. She didn't know what it was but something was nagging at her. She left Venezuela and hopefully all the negativity it brought to her when she got home she felt a sense of relief a sense of calm. But the news she received when she arrived was something she couldn't take. It was the most horrible news she could've received her father was in a car accident. He passed away while she was gone.

CHAOS

While LT was in Venezuela her father was doing his regular errands. He was on his way to the city to pick up some special flowers for Lucinda's garden. He got into a horrific car accident on the George Washington bridge. Dean couldn't even console her. She just felt her heart breaking over and over. She knew where she had to go. She went to her mother. Lucinda didn't say a word she was still in shock.

"Mom how are you?. I'm sorry I wasn't here for you. How are you holding up." She asked Her mother. Lucinda said nothing. She just had a blank look on her face. She was still in disbelief the man she'd loved most of her life was gone. He wasn't coming back ever. When she finally snapped out of the trance she was in she hugged LT tightly. She said "you're all I have left now". Latanya felt that in her soul. The two women held one another and cried.

The funeral arrangements were made by LT. She wouldn't let her mother take on anymore stress. Dean did everything he could to take some of the burden off of the two ladies. He lost a friend and a father in law. When it was time for the wake Lucinda saw friends she hadn't seen in years. She was a little relieved that she didn't have to do this alone. All the stories everyone had about Linden brought a sense of joy to her.

Her friends were telling everyone the story of how they met and how she became his Goldilocks. She hadn't heard that in years. LT also enjoyed hearing all the stories about her father. Some from before she was born and others she'd forgotten. As Linden's cousins told stories of his childhood everyone gathered around.

That's when Dean received a call from a friend from bridges and tunnels he asked Lawrence to look over the footage from that day. He'd known Linden for a while and he knew he was a careful driver. He didn't suspect foul play until this phone call. "Are you sure that's what happened?" Dean asked Lawrence through the phone. "Ok thanks, I appreciate everything you've done." Dean hung up more confused than anything.

Lawrence had just told him it looked like he lost control out of nowhere like the brakes had been cut. But who would do this and why? Deans detective skills kicked in. He was on the case. When the funeral was over Dean decided to let LT and Lucinda know what he learned about Linden's death. He asked them both if they knew anyone who would want to hurt him. He went into full detective mode. LT instantly thought about Mario. She thought they'd settle there differences. She saw now that he wasn't taking no for an answer. He went to far and she was ready for revenge. She needed more details before she went forward.

When Dean got to the precinct the surveillance was waiting for him. Jessica already looked at it but watched it again with Dean. Linden was driving fine then the car spiralled out of control, out of nowhere. When the car was inspected they saw the break lines were indeed cut. But who would do that as far as Dean knew he was just a truck driver. This was taking his mind off of Monroe for awhile but he needed justice for his wife's father.

When Dean got home that evening LT was waiting to hear the news. She prayed it wouldn't have to get out of hand but Monroe was ready for whatever came next. When Dean told her the break lines were indeed tampered with she broke down. She couldn't believe the lifestyle she'd chose finally caught up to her. It caused her pain she couldn't live with. She knew a meeting with Monroe was going to happen.

When she was alone she called Monroe they then set up a meeting. This one hit them both hard. The line had been crossed.

Mario wanted a war and that is exactly what he was going to get. Monroe told LT to come to there safe house so they can discuss there plan of action. They didn't start a war but they sure were going to finish it. When LT got to Monroe they both agreed they had to strike back. Monroe had been in the business longer. So this was nothing new. They decided they would send in Winston. He'd been Monroe's henchman since the business started. LT only saw him two times since she'd been in the business. She knew exactly what this meant. The problem will be taken care of. She carried on with business as usual.

She went back to work everyone there was trying to console her but she didn't want to talk about it. She was just waiting on word from Monroe. She knew what she had to do. They'd set up a meeting with Mario to try and settle this. The way LT was feeling she felt like she'd kill him on sight. But Monroe had a different approach. Monroe decided they'd take over Mario's business then deal with him after. Monroe was looking at the bigger picture.

LT had to pretend she wanted to work with Mario. She'd change her mind. No one knew about Linden's accident officially. As far as everyone was concerned it was just an accident nothing more nothing less. Mario underestimated LT. He also forgot she married a detective. She never really wanted Dean involved in her side business because the case involved her dad he tried to keep her a little updated on all leads.

Dean was hitting dead ends everywhere he turned. Linden was clean so he didn't see why there was foul play. Who could've done this. He decided to turn his focus to Monroe. He was under the radar for a while. There was no movement on his part. Jessica walked in and said an old partner from the Dominican Republic had informed her that the crime boss Mario was starting a war with Monroe. He'd hit three shipments of Monroe's. A war was brewing and Dean was ready to take everyone down.

LT got in touch with Mario and set up the meeting. When she got there it took everything in her not to kill him where he stood. Monroe made it very clear what was to be done. The long game is what was being played. "Mario I've had Change of heart, Monroe wants to do things the old fashion way. I'm ready to take my talents to another level. I want to expand but Monroe is comfortable with what we have going. I'm ready." LT said holding back her anger.

"I was hoping you'd come around beautiful." He said while moving the hair from her face to behind her ears. "Listen business is business I'm married so I'd appreciate if you'd respect that." She said with a hint of disgust. Then she smiled to cover up the way she really felt about him. He understood he really wanted her on his team so he had to respect what she said. That was the day LT left Monroe and started a business relationship with her mortal enemy.

MONROE

Lucinda was born in a small village called seventy two miles potaro in Guyana. She didn't come from a wealthy family. Her father was a taxi driver in Georgetown. He was well known. He even drove the prime ministers daughter around a few times. Sydney was the man to call if you wanted a luxury ride. Lucinda's mother Jewel was a kind soul. She was a headmistress at Saint Rose's high school. All of the children at the school was afraid of her but loved her at the same time.

Lucinda had two older brothers Junior and Lee. They were very overprotective of their little sister. She was always getting into fights because the other little girls were jealous of her. All the boys had crushes on her. She mostly stayed to herself. Lucinda enjoyed writing and playing football with the boys. Girls weren't exactly lining up to be her friend. She was a pretty tomboy so the guys gravitated towards her.

When she became a teenager she started selling pickled mango and chicken foot after school. She was a natural born hustler. She would sell it from 2pm-7pm. Then her father would pick her up. He was her biggest investor. He saw the way his daughter handled her business. At sixteen she was making enough money to buy her own clothes and whatever else she wanted. He taught her well she caught on fast with anything thrown her way.

One day Sydney had a meeting in town so he decided to take Lucinda along. His sons never had the drive that she did so he decided to include her in his other job. That job was Gold trading. When she got Into the factory she couldn't believe her eyes. There was gold everywhere. She was amazed at how her father spoke so

77

sternly to the men. She had never seen her father in that light. What would've scared any girl off excited her. She knew she wanted to be a boss like her father.

When the meeting was over and they were on their way home Lucinda had so many questions for her father. " so daddy you's da big boss?" Her accent was so heavy her father couldn't help but laugh. "I'm one of them" Sydney replied in a smooth tone. He knew her interest was peaked if he was going to leave his business to anyone it would be his daughter. Just watching her sell her mangos and how she didn't take anything from anyone he knew it would be left in good hands.

Lucinda's dad passed away when she was just twenty seven. But before he did he showed her the ins and outs of the business. She was running things smoothly by the age of thirty. She knew the men wouldn't take her serious so she brought in some muscle. Her childhood friend Winston. She was the face and he was the protection. He kept her safe they'd been best friends since primary school. He didn't speak much he was the observer.

When Lucinda first brought LT in on her business she told her it would one day be hers. "Listen I getting old so you gonna tek over one day". She explained to LT. " I have rules always refer to me as Monroe. Any meeting any phone call I'm a man. When I came to America that's what I called myself after my dad died I took over and I've used our last name. The associates all think I'm a man. That's the persona I've taken on. It gets the job done men don't want a woman to be a boss. I realized that and created Monroe.

LT loved the idea of her mom being a bad ass boss. She never did her own runs. By the time she got to America she had loyal workers who followed her rules. LT was groomed from birth to become the next boss. Her mother wanted nothing but the best for her. So when she decided to marry Dean a detective Lucinda had reservations. She was right to but her daughter had made up her mind and LT got her stubborn attitude from her father.

When LT met with her mom to discuss how they would deal with Mario. She saw a darkness in her mother she'd never seen before. She thought her heart was broken but she watched her mother slip into a dark place that she may not ever come back from. They devised their plan but Lucinda always had a back up plan in play. She hadn't ever gotten her hands dirty but this was personal Extremely personal.

She sent LT in to gather as much intel as possible. She told LT she would tell Mario she needed a bigger role in the business and Monroe wasn't trying to hear it. So she left and now they would bring Monroe down together. While LT was basically undercover Lucinda sent out frank he was her second best "employee".

No one in the organization knew what was going on between Monroe and LT but they knew a war was coming. A few months into her double life LT got to know how Mario thought and moved. She was ready to bring all the intel back to Monroe. When they met up LT hugged her mother and got right to it. "Mom he's ready to attack. He feels like he won by getting me on his side he has a shipment coming in on Friday that would be the best time to move on him.

Dean was still on the case. He'd heard Monroe lost his main runner to a rival named Mario. He felt as though it was almost over. He was going to take everyone down in the whole ring. Jessica's old partner in the Dominican Republic had gotten word that a shipment would be arriving in the country on friday. This was the lead Dean needed. Captain Casey gave the two the go ahead and they were booked and ready to head there.

When Dean got home he told LT he'd be going to the Dominican Republic to follow a lead. When she realized it was the same shipment she'd be apart of she had to think fast on how she'd get out of it and how to warn Mario to move the location. She hated the fact that Dean was investigating the people she worked for. The fact that Dean would be there as well made things a little difficult.

LT told Monroe about the location change she was excited because she knew people in that area and it would be easier to get to

Mario and end this once and for all. She told LT to stay in America. This was something Monroe had to settle on her own. LT didn't want to defy her mother so she did as she was told. Sitting home waiting for word on what was going down was driving LT crazy so she decided to go see her god daughter Star. She was the only person who could take LT's mind off of the things going on in her life.

LT got to Ariels as soon as she got home from picking Star up from school. Star ran into LT's arms. "Auntie LT I've missed you so much." Star said while smiling. LT never had baby fever this strong until now. She realized she wanted a child of her own. She kissed Star on the cheek and pulled out a pink teddy bear out of her pocketbook and gave it to her god daughter. "I missed you too muffin" LT said while walking into the house with Ariel and Star. She had to take her mind off of the meeting that was taking place that she was missing.

Ariel sensed something was off with LT and asked her "what's going on girl?" LT couldn't tell her the real reason so she decided to tell her she was ready for children. These were the words Ariel had been waiting to hear for years. "Does Dean know. When will you start trying have you started already?" Ariel bombarded LT with questions. LT smiled and told her "when Dean gets back from the Dominican Republic I'll talk to him about it. He's been ready since day one girl." The two laughed.

While Ariel made dinner LT sat there drinking a glass of wine. She got really mellow and relaxed. That was until she received a text from Monroe.

It's happening now, I'll see you when I get back

LT was anxious and nervous to see how this would play out but for now she'd sit back and enjoy her friends company and dinner. She decided to spend time with Ariel and have a tea party with Star. This was the distraction she needed.

CALM

Dean and Jessica arrived in the Dominican Republic Thursday evening to set up surveillance where they thought the meeting would be. While they did their stakeout Jessica began to tell Dean about her plans. "I'm ready to get married partner. I saw how you and LT were at your wedding and it just made me feel something. There was so much love there." She said to him while looking at the monitors.

He thought about LT before he answered her. " Listen when you love someone you just know. I see how you are with Nalini and how she is with you. You two are perfect for one another you have my blessing." He said while laughing and touching her shoulder.

They sat in front of an abandoned building for twelve hours. Dean felt like there should've been more movement than that. He told Jessica to call her man on the inside. When he finally answered he told her the location was changed last minute. Dean was pissed to say the least. They both scrambled to secure the equipment because they had to be across town. Dean decided to drive he had a mission to complete he just knew he'd face off with Monroe he could feel it.

On the other side of town Mario was preparing to meet the man they called Monroe. He knew Monroe was angry he took his best worker LT. He tightened security because he didn't know what to expect. Jose stayed close by he made sure his boss was covered in every aspect. The one thing they didn't consider is that Monroe didn't only have LT undercover. There were several men who infiltrated Mario's operation. This was going to be a showdown one that wouldn't end well for many involved.

As Winston drove Monroe to the drop she made him stop at a flower shop. She picked up a bouquet of flowers. Victorian lilies is what she decided on because it was Guyana's national flower. It meant the end for Mario. She was saying her goodbyes. When Lucinda was twenty minutes from the meeting she called LT. "Hey baby girl, I'm almost there I wanted to call and check in and let you know this maybe the last time we speak." Lucinda spoke those cold words into the phone.

LT thought it would just be a meeting. She didn't know her mom planned on ending things officially. "Mom what are you saying? Don't do whatever it is you plan on doing please." LT pleaded. She knew from the tone in her mother's voice she meant every word of what she was saying. She looked at the phone and a flood of tears streamed down her face. She knew a day like this would come but she didn't think it would be so soon. She never even got to give her parents grandchildren her heart broke all over again.

When Winston pulled up he asked Monroe if she was ready. She responded "more than I've ever been". Winston got out and opened the door for her and they walked in. When they finally made it inside Mario was sitting at the table awaiting their arrival. He thought Winston was Monroe until he saw Lucinda sit at the table. "Wait a minute, wait a minute you're the infamous Monroe." Mario questioned. He was in total shock.

Lucinda sat there with a blank stare on her face. She wasn't in the mood for questions. "Yes that's me now let's carry on with business." She said. Mario thought she was there to discuss a truce. He wanted all the territories but he was willing to leave her a small piece. He'd already taken LT so he knew she took a hit with that one.

"Mario do you know who I am?" Lucinda questioned. Mario sat with a confused look on his face. Not really sure how to answer. "No should I know who you are" he said with a thick accent. "Let me tell you then, my husband was on his way to get flowers. These flowers here." She said laying the flowers on the table. That's when Mario put it together she was LT's mother she was Monroe. He'd been set up. "Well isn't this clever send in your daughter to spy

Well played Monroe well played." He said while smiling. "But you've come to me to do what exactly? You're here to whine about your dead husband. You brought one old man with you." He said laughing loudly. "You're as dumb as you look. I've been in this business before you were born. I wouldn't show who I am without backup."

That's when five of Mario's men pulled their guns out and turned them on him and the men Monroe didn't hire. Jose drew his gun trying to protect his boss but Winston already had his drawn. It was a standoff. Mario couldn't stop laughing. He couldn't believe what was happening. His own men turning on him. Monroe stood up and walked over to him and said "I promised myself I'd kill you." When she pulled the twenty two out her holster someone burst in the door.

"Freeze everyone weapons down." Dean came in with his gun drawn. He was in shock when he saw his mother in law with a gun to a gangsters head. That's when Jose shot Lucinda and she went down. Winston let off five shots into Jose. A gun fight erupted. That's when Mario ducked and tried to get out. Dean started firing. Mario ran out the back door while Dean ran over to Lucinda. Jessica was in pursuit of Mario.

Dean applied pressure to the wound and tried to keep Lucinda alive. As she laid in his arms gasping for air. "Keep calm Lucinda, keep calm" he repeated. How could he tell his wife her mother was a mobster. "Lucinda hold on you're going to be ok". Dean said while calling for help. Winston was also trying to catch Mario. That was the mission to end him. Jessica came back and didn't know what to say. She called the ambulance but Lucinda bled out before they could get there. Dean just held his lifeless mother in law and cried. He didn't think that catching Monroe would end like this.

THE FINALE

As LT sat around waiting for an update she felt this gut wrenching pain in her stomach. That feeling you get when something terribly wrong has happened. She didn't know what to do. She knew she couldn't call her mother so she just sat and waited. A few hours later she received a call from Winston telling her the story of what had happened.

She instantly felt sick. She ran to the bathroom and threw up immediately. Her mother was gone is all that kept replaying in her head. She knew what she had to do there was always a protocol in place if something ever happened to Monroe. She reached out to all her contacts and updated them all.

It was a sad day in the gold industry. When Dean finally got around to calling her she had to pretend it was her first time hearing the news. Deans heart broke through the phone telling his wife her mother was gone. As he told her a tear fell down his face because he couldn't be there to console her. He then realized her mother was Monroe and went into detective mode. "LT did you know? Did you know who your mother was?" He questioned. Lucinda always told LT never let anyone know who you really are.

"No Dean if I did she'd still be alive." She said crying into the phone. She had another call coming in so she told Dean she needed a moment to herself. Winston was on her line telling her he had eyes on Mario. She wanted to be there when he paid for what he did to her parents so she told Winston to grab him. Winston had been in the military in Guyana so being stealth was no problem.

He was ready to handle the situation because he just lost his nearest and dearest friend. But he knew LT deserved to at least watch the man that murdered her parents get what he deserved. After he grabbed Mario he brought him back to America on Monroe's private jet. He was going to make him pay.

When LT got the call the next day to meet up she already knew what it meant. Dean wasn't getting in until the following day so she had time to go handle her business. When she arrived at the warehouse in the Bronx it smelled like burning meat. Winston had already started on Mario.

He had his torture kit out. He'd already tied Mario up and bash his face with brass knuckles. Winston was old school. He liked physical contact he wasn't really into the fast death. He'd also had a cutlass he cut Mario twenty five times already. The handsome Venezuelan looked like a tortured POW.

When LT saw him she threw up. She figured it was because she hadn't really witnessed something so violent up close. She'd soon find out that wasn't the case. When she walked in Winston stepped aside. She came face to face with the man that killed her parents. All he could say was "I can make this right what do you want?" Mario pleaded.

LT stood over him and screamed "I WANT MY FUCKING PARENTS BACK" as she started swinging on him. Winston had to pull her off of him. She got a hold of herself and went back to Mario. "A thousand deaths wouldn't be enough for you". She said with disgust oozing from her voice. You took my parents from me now your life is mine. An eye for an eye Mario. You started a war that I'm going to finish. "Winston end this piece of shit". She said with venom dripping from her words.

Winston held the cutlass and in one swift motion he decapitated Mario. The once handsome man that could have been Antonio Sabàto Jr's twin was now a lifeless headless corpse. LT ran off and threw up again. Winston knew something she didn't. She was pregnant. "Latanya when you leave here go get a pregnancy test." He said with a raised brow. She looked at him as though he had two heads. "Uncle Winston you're insane I'm not pregnant this is just disgusting. I've never been around for this part" she said wiping puke from her lips.

"Listen I remember when your mother was pregnant with you. It was the same story, every second she deh throwing up." He said with his Guyanese accent he didn't lose all those years in America. With everything going on LT didn't even remember she hadn't had a period since her honeymoon. She thought wow it's something about honeymoons the same thing happened to Ariel.

She hugged Winston and asked him what was next. He replied "baby girl I'm tired we knew it would end one day I just wish it was different." He hugged LT and kissed her and told her again to find out if she was pregnant. She told him she would and she left so he could clean up the garbage that was Mario.

When she got to her car she couldn't stop shaking and crying. Her hands still had Mario's blood on them. She drove to the nearest rite aid and got a clear blue pregnancy test. She didn't want to believe what Winston was saying but now she was curious.

When she got home she showered first she had to get the blood off of her. She looked at her fist they were swollen. She got mad all over again and punched the walls. Just in case Dean asked why they were swollen. She'd tell him she was angry from the news of her mother. Lucinda always told her to cover all bases. When LT got out the shower she dried herself off and sat on the bed staring at the test. It was now or never her future stared her right in the face and she honestly didn't want to know. She fell asleep before she could take the test.

The next morning when LT woke up Dean was sitting on the edge of the bed holding the test in his hand. LT jumped up and told him she was afraid to take it alone. When she finally mustered up the courage to get out of bed Dean was right on her heels. She had to turn around and tell him she had it from here as she closed the bathroom door in his face. She didn't really have time to think about a baby with everything that was going on. Just yesterday she lost her mother and watched the man that killed her parents die. It was to much she just sat on the toilet crying.

Dean was impatient he wanted to know if he'd be a father so he knocked. That knock got LT out of the trance she was in. She finally peed on the stick and waited. She told Dean he could come in and read what the results were. He rushed in the lines weren't formed yet so he told her she wasn't pregnant. She just looked at him and the tears flowed. He then looked at the test again and two pink lines appeared. "LT what does these two lines mean" he asked with his eyes locked on the test. "Babe we're pregnant" she answered with a glimmer of hope. He threw the test and grabbed Latayna's face and kissed her passionately.

At this moment Dean didn't care about anything, Monroe or the case nothing mattered. The woman he loved was going to give him a child. How could he tell his wife he suspected she had involvement in a gold bartering ring. He had a choice to make and he chose love. He didn't want to know. His wife had loss so much he couldn't bring himself to ruin this moment. This was the life he wanted his happy ending.